DRAGON'S MOUTH

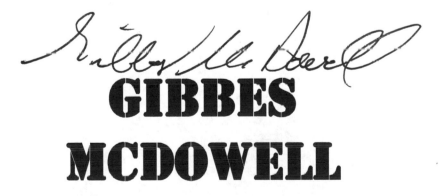

GIBBES

MCDOWELL

GIBBES McDOWELL

DRAGON'S MOUTH

GIBBES McDOWELL

ISBN-13: 978-1-7349515-9-2

YBR PUBLISHING, LLC

Jack Gannon – Co-Owner, Production Manager
Cyndi Williams-Barnier – Co-Owner, Production Editor
Bill Barnier – Co-Owner, Senior Editor
Loreen Ridge-Husum – Art Director
Michelle Owens – Marketing Agent

DRAGON'S MOUTH

ALSO BY THE AUTHOR:

Driftwood Unmasked

DRAGON'S MOUTH

Dedicated to my loving wife, Fleetwood.

DRAGON'S MOUTH

ACKNOWLEGEMENTS

My gratitude to YBR Publishing, and to my Editors, Bill and Cyndi Barnier, cannot be overstated. Without their disciplined guidance, intuition, and enthusiasm for this project, it would not be the remarkable story it has become.

And not least to thank are the active duty and retired military officers from the United States Marine Corps, United States Army, and United States Navy who are graciously embraced in credits, for their invaluable contributions to plot cohesion, military hardware, tactics, and language that drive this story.

DRAGON'S MOUTH

REVIEWS

"A Great thriller. Very believable story. Super characters come alive and suited for the task at hand. This could be real."

~CW04 Charles L. Jones (US Marine Corps)

"A mix of fact and fiction sure to capture a wide range of readers. Well researched and excellent use of assets."

~Lt. Justin Besinger (US Navy SEAL)

"A chilling yet compelling read in that the entire epic coherently connects a number of actual and possible, related and yet sometimes disparate, events that in the end are linked to the survival of this nation. Most sinister is that linkage is through a single anti-hero, an ISIS fighter."

~Colonel George B. Utter (US Army Ranger)

"*Dragon's Mouth* is as good as any spook adventure I've ever read. Move over Tom Clancy."

~Author Roger Pinckney XI

Review By Lex Allen for Readers' Favorite"

All roads lead to Yellowstone National Park in this action-packed novel from Gibbes McDowell. Dragon's Mouth is a non-stop thriller complete with Navy SEALS, the FBI, and an Al Qaeda terrorist planning an attack on the United States that will make 9-11 look like child's play. This story mixes intrigue, action, a touch of romance, and a startling conclusion that could easily be a portent of tomorrow's headlines.

Gibbes McDowell writes lies, good lies as described in Stephen King's quote, "Fiction is a lie. Good fiction is the truth within the lie." He writes these lies in a way that makes all the pieces of the plotline... in the case of Dragon's Mouth, three major plotlines... the characters, and all the supporting nuts and bolts of storytelling come alive with a strong dose of verisimilitude; a big word for "sense of reality." McDowell is adept at weaving the stories and harrowing missions of Navy SEALs AC and Toad, their combined yet unrequited love for Dr. Christie Albright, the never say quit FBI Agent Dan Shield, and the Al Qaeda terrorist Kamal as well as a host of supporting actors, into a tight story of page-turning intensity. Dragon's Mouth could be the next headline story to capture global attention—it's that realistic!

Either through personal experience or exceptional research and advisors, McDowell displays a level of expertise in weaponry, terrorist and US military tactics, and the inner workings of the FBI in a manner so that even the less knowledgeable reader will be drawn into the story with complete cognition. Together with a writing style and a keen sense of timing in the use of real-world events,

McDowell lures the reader into a trap that will not release until the last page is read. The conclusion of this story is complete, with no strings left untied; but there is still a hint of a sequel. I certainly hope so. In conclusion: if you're a fan of military fiction, tales of action and adventure, or simply edge-of-your-seat thrillers, you'll love Gibbes McDowell's Dragon's Mouth!

DRAGON'S MOUTH

This book is a work of fiction. Names, places, characters, and dialogues are the product of the author's imagination. Any similarity to establishments, persons, locales, or actual events is entirely coincidental.

DRAGON'S MOUTH

TABLE OF CONTENTS

DRAGON'S MOUTH

PROLOGUE

In the time of man, a place of exquisite beauty and grandeur would come to be called Yellowstone. A beast of primordial power sleeps beneath…

"And I saw three unclean spirits, like frogs, come out of the Mouth of the Dragon, and out of the mouth of the Beast, and out of the mouth of false prophets."

~Revelations 16:13.

"…Mr. President, within the hour the entire world will know if there is going to be any North American tomorrow…"

CHAPTER 1: DEAD BONES

At the glacial pace of celestial time, the Pacific tectonic plate had been sub-ducting beneath the North American tectonic plate, wrinkling the earth's surface and pushing the resulting debris pile into large rocky ridges which in later eons would be known as the Rocky Mountains. Miles below the surface the tremendous heat and pressure of such titanic motions fired a molten process that would melt inward through the earth's mantle to its inner core, releasing plumes of molten lava that pushed and forced its way through cracks and crevasses to the surface, breaking out in sporadic thunderous eruptions of molten rock, ash, and steam.

Continent building is a messy business. In the wake of early creation remains a permanent volcanic tap into the planet's molten core. Centered roughly beneath the western third of the new continent, this feature is the largest of its kind in all the world; sulking, churning, angry at its pressured confinement, venting its anger in fits of steam and shooting geysers as would a fitful Dragon of yore.

Relentless pressure would ultimately have its day. That day last came 640,000 years ago.

The bucolic scene of a great plain above the caldron, lush with tall green grass and sparkling clear streams, was populated with herds of mega-fauna. Antelope and giant buffalo numbering in the tens of thousands grazed peacefully. The Woolly Rhinoceros strutted his brute strength, bullied his way to the choicest feed but being careful not to provoke the eighteen-inch sickle-like claws of a two-ton giant ground sloth munching stream side treetops. And from atop a crusty termite mound sat a pair of hungry Saber-Toothed cats, ever watchful for signs of weakness and an easy meal.

Then some sixth sense brought all to a stop. The primordial beast beneath their feet began to stir. The ground began to tremble and shake. Feeling a creeping, blanketing uneasiness, milling buffalo panicked in wide eyed terror; great herds stampeding in aimless desperation. The sleepy Rhino watched through dull, ignorant eyes. Great cracks opened in the ground, cross stitching the landscape for fifty miles in every direction, swallowing the daylight world into the abyss. Mile high walls of flame, smoke, and molten rock belched skyward as the earth heaved, split, and tumbled into itself. Hell's acrid burning breath belched forth. With a great thundering roar on a scale never known to human eyes or ears, the earth vomited molten chunks of planetary innards into near space orbit. The force of the blast squeezed and compressed the air at ground zero into a racing wall of fire and destruction expanding from its epicenter at supersonic speeds; compressed so tightly that the very air caught fire, incinerating everything in its path. The wall of death scalped the eastern face of the Rocky Mountains down to its bare granite bones. Forests and grasslands vaporized in an instant. Terrified wildlife was overcome by the blast, charred, and torn asunder before their dead bodies could fall to the ground. Every living thing and the topsoil on which they stood, within a thousand-mile radius of the eruption was incinerated, gone in an instant.

For months after the blast a gentle suffocating snow-like blanket of death fell upon the earth, upon the scoured dead bones of all that had come before.

CHAPTER 2: THE INFIDELS

Fatwa: Osama bin Laden:

"The ruling to kill the Americans and their allies, civilian and military, is the individual duty of every Muslim who can do it in any country in which is it possible to do it. This, in accordance with the words of Almighty God who said to fight the pagans all together as they fight you all together. And fight them until there is no more tumult or oppression, and there prevails justice and faith in God."

A golden Arabian moon casts a glow upon a sullen gray brute. One hundred thousand gross tons and a quarter million nuclear horsepower of American sovereignty slowly turned into the wind in preparation for battle. The USS Nimitz, stationed in the Red Sea, was the largest and deadliest aircraft carrier in the United States arsenal, a hammer of freedom against the nail of anarchy. Untethered from land-based constraints, the Nimitz carrier strike group was free to bypass regional politics and display American resolve like no other asset in the nation's war chest.

On the pre-dawn flight deck crews of sailors, in job distinct code colored float coats, performed their choreographed arming and fueling of aircraft in preparation for flight operations. No wasted time, no unprofessional action. The tools of freedom and those who fly them deserved nothing less.

And in the pilots' Ready Room below the flight deck, anxious flight crews gathered for a briefing.

While the communications room and navigation center are the heart of the Nimitz, the Ready Room is its soul. Eager testosterone junkies, cocky and self-assured, aggressively mocked each other in the brotherhood language unique to fighter pilots; a bond that enabled them to dismiss death's daily entreaties.

Where the rest of the Nimitz is covered in dull navy gray paint, the Ready Room's walls sport the colors and insignia of the flight group gathered for that day's mission brief. A large white board heads the room where battle plans and men's lives are choreographed into the cold, hard mechanics of combat aviation. All in attendance sat in rows of leather-bound steel chairs bolted to the deck. Fold away desktops and note pads record each man's part of the larger battle plan.

"Hey, Rooster, what's up?"

"The CAG called a meeting," Major AC "Rooster" Collins replied in a pensive mood.

"D'ya score that French chic back in Toulon?"

"Hell yeah, banged her bowlegged."

Lieutenant Ross Roberts, call sign Migs, chimed in. "That toothy brunette? She could chew corn through a picket fence. I wouldn't do her with Mike's dick."

Across the Ready Room, Mike returned fire. "Hey, I can do my own screwing, thank you."

Then all heads turned toward the hatch to the Ready Room when the Executive Officer (XO) for the VMFA barked, "Attention on deck!"

The Commander Air Group (CAG) prepared to address a Ready Room full of pilots nursing last night's hangovers, their mugs of steaming black coffee challenged red-rimmed eyes and sore heads.

Wandering eyes caught four Blues in a back corner of the room.

A junior pilot, noting the squadron patches on their chests, spouted off from his rung in the jet jockey pecking order, whispering to the guy on his 10 o'clock. "What the fuck are those Air Force A-10 drivers doing here?"

He was cut short by the CAG.

27

"Good morning, gentlemen. Until five days ago, the Nimitz appeared to be in standby mode. That's not exactly what's been going on. Since day one, the details of this mission have been on a need-to-know basis. Until now, you didn't need to know. Now that we're on the ball, I'm going to read you in.

"One month ago, US intelligence discovered a plot by a rogue Saudi general to overthrow the Saudi regime for a more radical, extremist sharia wing of Islam. This is a national strategic event, and it is scheduled to execute two days from today.

"General Ahmed Ibrahim and a loyal staff of junior officers used a fake training exercise to steal an entire armored division of Saudi tanks, half-tracks, mobile missile launchers, SAMS, and 1,000 battle-hardened troops from the Saudi regime. He has hidden them deep off the map in a deserted, lawless no-man's-land beyond government control. His command center is housed in a reinforced thousand-year-old fortress, a forgotten relic from the Crusades. Hidden beneath the sands of the Arabian desert and lost to modern history, this fort was recently unearthed by a fierce sandstorm known to locals in the area as a haboob. Our NSA satellites have been re-tasked to keep eyes on this operation, while ground based Intel also reports that General Ibrahim has been secretly provisioning and reinforcing this outpost for the past six months. He is acting under orders from a prince inside the Saudi crown family to topple the House of Saud."

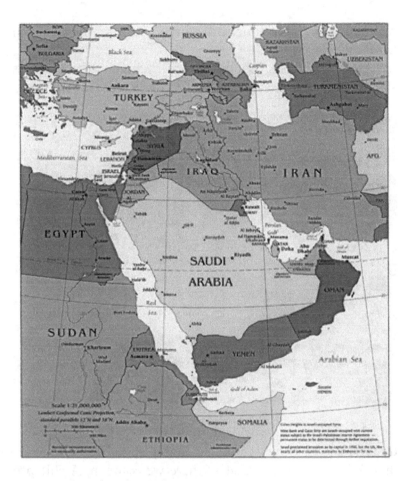

A couple of mumbled "holy shits" and "mother fuckers" were heard floating about the room.

The CAG continued. "In two days, there is scheduled to be a Top-Secret multilateral trade and security meeting by Saudi and Qatar leadership at the palace of a Qatar Prince. Look at your maps. An intercepted communication between General Ibrahim and his sponsors details a plan to kill these negotiations and decapitate Saudi leadership with a two-hundred-mile night-time full force surprise attack from across the desert.

"The traitorous Saudi Prince behind this coup is standing ready to assume control of the Saudi Government.

"In the Saudi world, family cannot kill family for transgressions. However, they can pay somebody else to do their killing for them. That's where we come in. A collapse of the Saudi Government would be catastrophic for regional stability and the United States would lose its strongest ally in the Middle East. If this coup is allowed to succeed, Russia, Syria, and Iran would rush in to fill the resulting power vacuum.

"The Saudis have, through the most discreet channels, asked us, their only ally with the assets to pull this off, to destroy this rogue general and his army. Off the record, no fingerprints tying the House of Saud to this action, no survivors, no questions asked. What we are about to do never happened. Is that understood?

"Turn to your target folders, gentlemen. Major AC Collins, call sign Rooster, will brief you on the strike plan code named Operation Conundrum. This comes straight from the Chairman of Joint Chiefs (CJCS). Our window of opportunity is at hand gentlemen. All slack has been removed from the trigger. AC?"

"Aye, Sir!"

Major Collins began his brief.

"Ten days of high-level planning, resupply in Toulon, France, and a three-day transit through the Suez Canal, and the North Red Sea brings us to our present location. Strike plan: Operation Conundrum is now hot. The CAG explained the international situation we are tasked with resolving. Some of you may be wondering why we need piloted aircraft for this mission, when Tomahawks and conventional cruise missiles could do the same job. This strike is like no other you will fly. For outside eyes and ears, we are not really here. Conundrum never happened. You will have only four minutes under electronic umbrella over the target to destroy General Ahmed Ibrahim's attempted coup, then disappear. As much as I hate to give credit to a hungover bunch of speed junkies, only human eyes, and pilot flexibility to change the battle plan in real time, can mean the difference between mission success or failure. Failure is not an option. That is why we're here, gentlemen.

"We're also way out of the box on this one. You will note some additional assets on board for this strike. You F-18 jocks will have to play nice with the HAWGS."

A flurry of questions and raised hands interrupted AC.

"Yeah, Migs, what you got?"

31

"Sir. A-10s are land based. What are they doing on our flight deck? And once airborne, they can't return to the Nimitz. They got no gear for a deck landing. I've flown a hundred combat sorties and never needed their help before."

"The HAWGS are on the flight deck because the Joint Chiefs J3, who writes your paycheck, says so. Straight from the top. He served as a First Lieutenant in Desert Storm in 1991, and as Battalion Commander in Iraqi Freedom, and again in Afghanistan. This guy pounded enough desert sand to move the Sahara to Florida in his three tours of this shit. He saw the A-10 in action up close and personal, says A-10s saved his ass in close combat situations a dozen times. He sold the A-10 to his boss, the four-star Chairman of Joint Chiefs, who directed Central Command to make it happen. Though the Navy pitched a bitch about including the A-10 in this strike plan, we all know shit rolls downhill; so here we are gentlemen. The special capabilities of the A-10 are why they are aboard the Nimitz. Four of 'em trucked on flatbeds to Port in the Med and craned aboard while most of you guys were sleeping off that whore house in Toulon. Pointing to the "Blues" in the back of the room, AC added, "their pilots were flown aboard two days ago."

An "HOO-YAH" rattled the Ready Room. Even the CAG cracked a smile thinking to himself, gotta stay loose, especially when your ass is in the sling.

"I know you F-18 guys don't want to hear it, but the truth is: The A-10 is unequaled when it comes to busting tanks, heavy armor on the move, and smaller targets of opportunity you fast movers can't slow down enough to kill. General Ibrahim's rogue army cannot survive this strike. The J3 intends to kill every last mother's son of 'em.

If the J3 wants A-10s on his boat, he gets A-10s on the boat. Anyone else?"

Call sign "Spikes" raised his hand.

"A-10s have never based on a carrier before. Their airspeed is half the F-18's. That mismatch seriously compounds targeting, refueling, and overall planning objectives. It's just never been done before."

"Tell that to Colonel Jimmy Doolittle."

"Sir?"

"You do know your military history, don't you?"

"I'm not following you, AC."

"The Doolittle Raid against Tokyo at the beginning of World War II. Nobody thought Doolittle could launch the B-24 off the carrier Hornet until he proved he could do it, maintaining the element of surprise. Doolittle didn't plan on returning to the Hornet and neither do our A-10's intend to return to the Nimitz. No other aircraft can 'chew the bone' like the A-10. Spitting seventy rounds per second from its seven barreled, 30mm Gatling gun, its depleted uranium armor piercing incendiary rounds are a fucking nightmare to enemy armor. The HAWGS can take care of themselves on route to a safe runway outside the operational umbrella."

An F-18 pilot turned to the Blues in the corner and commented, "Gutsy move, dudes."

Several other nodding heads around the Ready Room and a couple of thumbs up cleared the air on the A-10 issue. They were all on the same page.

"Anybody else?"

Apparently unmoved by the hurried standby status were two Saudi pilots trained at Pensacola under the Navy's international pilot training program. On temporary loan from the Saudi Government and assigned to the Nimitz, they sat stoically, taking it all in. Typically, sons of a wealthy sheik, politician, or member of a royal family, they exude a superior arrogance not tolerated in other training programs, the price of international diplomacy. They stay to themselves and are regarded with some suspicion by U.S. pilots. After all, it was Saudi pilots trained in a Florida flight school who flew three commercial airliners into the Twin Towers in New York City and the Pentagon on 9/11.

"Moving on. An MV-22 Osprey inserted SEAL Team Six five clicks from the target yesterday. They maneuvered into position atop this ridge overlooking the target."

Using his laser pointer on the power point screen, AC explained the target area.

"Central command is the old Crusader fort and communications tower. Satellite recon has located SAM sites here, here, and here. Temporary troop barracks are nestled under this ridgeline. Armored formations are a moving target.

"Our SEALS will be laser painting the hard targets for the F-18s that will take them out with thousand-pound laser guided ordinance. The EA-6B and HARMS (High Speed Anti-Radiation Missiles) fired from F-18s will suppress enemy air defense. Four minutes over the target and gone. The A-10s, call signs Wolf 1, Wolf 2, Wolf 3, and Wolf 4 will follow the main strike before any defensive response can be organized. They are tasked with cleaning up any remaining armor, targets of opportunity, and any surviving wigglers and squirters. I want to catch these camel jockeys with their pants down.

"On a note of irony, you gentlemen may appreciate; our Department of Defense recently sold the legitimate Saudi military thirty brand new Abrams tanks for the tidy sum of $1.5 billion. Now we're about to shoot the shit out of our own equipment, which General Ibrahim stole from the Saudis. Go figure."

An anonymous pilot in the back of the Ready Room mumbled, "That's fucked up, man."

"Back to the business at hand," AC continued without reply.

"A KC-135 fuel tanker will be on station at 10,000 feet at these coordinates, inbound and on your return. His call sign is Mother Jugs.

"Let's make this one count, in and out, clean and tight.

"Any questions?"

"Who's the SEAL Team commander on the ground?" asked an F-18 driver.

"What's his call sign if we have to adjust the battle plan?"

"That'd be Master Chief 'Toad' Rawlings; call sign 'Badger'."

"I've heard of that guy; a real hard ass, if you believe his rep."

AC took a deep breath and waved off the comment.

"Master Chief Rawlings is capable, and battle tested. If there are no more questions, I suggest you all get ready to rumble. 'H' hour is 0130 hours. Good luck, gentlemen. I'll see you back in CIC"--Combat Information Center-- "after the dance."

As the Ready Room briefing broke up, a cryptic note previously passed under table from one pilot to another fell from a pilot's clipboard to slip unnoticed to the floor between his seat and fold down desktop.

As H hour approached, all pilots checked personal gear, some leaving a "what if" letter to family on their bunks. Some took a knee in prayer, while others stoically went about preparations to execute their mission.

All hanger decks were an orchestrated chaos of moving aircraft, elevators bringing aircraft and munitions to hanger decks, engine noise, the queuing up of mission assets in their respective order of departure on the catapult deck.

At exactly zero-one-thirty hours the Nimitz was turned into the wind and the four A-10s took off in pairs, their turbines washing the flight deck in a beguiling "whoosh", deceptive of the firepower they possessed. Since they are not equipped for a catapult launch, the nimble Thunderbolts used their Short Takeoff and Landing (STOL) capability to self-launch from the short carrier deck.

The A-10s were quickly followed by the EA-6B Prowlers already in the catapult. They would provide the electronic cone of silence cloaking Operation Conundrum from detection by enemy forces.

An hour later the four F-18s roared off into the predawn light, pilot and navigator straddled atop thunderous, deck shaking after burners. They were followed by two F/A-18s whose job was to jam enemy targeting radar.

Four hours into Operation Conundrum each aircraft, in launch order, prepared to ease up to the underbelly of Mother Jugs to lock on to the drogue fuel line trailing out behind her for the extra twenty-five-hundred pounds of fuel needed to reach the target and return for refill.

Simultaneously, back on the Nimitz, a Seaman cleaning the Ready Room picked up a handwritten note not in English. About to toss it into the trash, a second impulse made him stuff it into his shirt pocket. Minutes later while signing off on his duty sheet, the sailor casually mentioned his find to a senior officer handing him the note. Startled by what he saw, he scrambled up to Intel.

Military prudence demands there be someone onboard who is fluent in the language native to the area of operations.

"Oh shit!" the translator shouted. "Get this to the CAG, ASAP."

One mile out from Mother Jugs, a secured transmission from the CAG aboard the Nimitz to Strike Leader Collins, ordered, "Splash Dash-4, the Saudi flown F/A-18."

"Sir?" questioned Collins.

"You heard me Rooster, execute! Shoot that spying terrorist mother fucker down."

With his finger on the trigger, Mother Jugs in his sights, and Allahu Akbar upon his lips, the Saudi piloted F-18 exploded in a massive, thirty-million-dollar fireball.

"Splashed Dash-4, sir."

"Acknowledged. Operation Conundrum is still a go."

The surviving strike force fueled up and moved on to target.

The F/A-18s and support caught up to the A-10s at the pre-arranged rendezvous point where Strike Leader Collins, miked the SEAL Team laser painting the Crusader fort, turned central compound.

"Badger, this is strike leader. We are at the rally point, inbound."

Badger's terse response, "That you, jarhead?"

Itching to return the barb, AC responded. "Just give me the Nine Line Badger. We'll do our job."

The other pilots and crew in the strike force just shook their heads at this non- S.O.P. exchange. "What the fu—"

Growling under his breath, Badger keyed the mike switch of his AN/PRC-152 handset while looking at his laminated 9-line briefing card where he'd scribbled the pertinent information of the target. "Abbreviated 9-line to follow."

"Lines 1, 2, 3, NA." Badger unkeyed his mike momentarily, then keyed it again in five more successive transmissions.

"Seven-zero meters,
Command Center,
N24 45.12 E38 02.45,
Laser, one-six-eight-eight,
East, two-zero-zero meters,
Egress southeast to check point Miller.
"Stand by for amplifying remarks."

AC entered the target elevation and LAT/LONG into his mission computer, tapping the keypad of the upfront control. "Ready for amplifying remarks."

Badger keyed his mike while looking through his binoculars. "TOT (time on target) zero-six-three-five. The target I gave you is the command post in the center of the compound. I want your first two LGBs targeted on that building. Dash-2, I want your two LGBs in the center of the armor formation parked just two hundred meters northeast of the command post. Dash-3/4, drop your remaining LGBs on the barracks fifty meters to the west of the command post."

AC and the pilots and crews of the other aircraft processed the 9-line and amplifying remarks. AC responded, "Copy 9-line."

Two minutes later, at time 0633, AC keyed his mike, "Inbound. We lost Dash-4 enroute."

With (ATFLIR), Advanced Targeting Forward Looking Infrared Radar, confirming targeting, the remaining three F-18s began their target run while the A-10s, loitering in a low altitude holding pattern, awaited their meal. Twenty miles and counting. From the EA-6B high and tight, an electronic blanket of silence began, causing nothing but "dead air" on the ground for anyone listening.

The Muslim call to morning prayer sounded from a minaret overlooking the terrorist compound in the early predawn. The rooster's crow pushed back the blanket of darkness, giving way to the morning sun rising full onto another desert day in no-man's-land. Nearly a thousand men began kneeling on prayer rugs, offering prayers to their maker.

Several cur dogs milling around suddenly turned toward the rising sun, ears perked, heads cocked sideways trying to make out a distant sound not part of their daily routine. Seconds later their masters heard it, too. Jumping to their feet, they shielded their eyes against the bright new sun, squinting to see through the glare.

Badger turned to his targeting team questioning; "Dash-4? How do you lose a fucking airplane? AC couldn't hit a bull in the butt with a baseball ba—" His sarcastic jab was cut short.

Before the terrorists could react, a great ripping, sucking sound presaged the delivery of guided heavy ordinance. The battle hardened among them, eyes white with fear, recognize the accelerating clickity-click sound of rear bomb fins making final targeting adjustments. WHAM, WHAM, WHAM. Six successive thousand-pound bombs dropped in pairs, two dead-center of the compound, two on the formations of heavy armor, and two on the troop barracks. The once gleaming white alabaster command center became a wrenched and bloodied hole in the ground. Even as the rubble from the main strike was still falling back to earth, the A-10 Warthogs were upon them. A hundred feet off the desert floor, angels of destruction materialized out of a shimmering desert mirage, their grinning cowl monikers the faces of death come a-calling. Inscribed around the muzzle of their main gun was the sobriquet "Smile when you see the flash".

"Ground Forces Command (GFC) to Wolf Pack. The field is yours. Light 'em up, boys."

Fighting in hungry pairs, the A-10's thirty-millimeter Gatling guns put a raping on what was left of the terrorists' compound. The first pass kneecapped a communication tower, bringing it down across the roof of an ancillary compound building and into the courtyard below.

Twisting and turning in a figure eight crossing pattern, each pilot covered his wingman's six, taking turns at nests of SAM bunkers. Tank crews, miscellaneous light armor, and pickup trucks with flatbed mounted heavy machine guns, scrambled to disburse. The lost munitions aboard the splashed F-18 left a target rich environment for the HAWGS. Torched and white-hot burning carcasses of charred iron and steel littered the landscape. Fuel tanks exploded in blistering balls of fire, billowing black plumes of smoke into the once pristine Arab dawn. Sporadic small arms fire and phosphorous green tracers laced the smoke-filled sky in a futile attempt to blunt the Infidel onslaught. The chainsaw BUZZZZZZZ of the HAWGS' Gatling guns silenced the most intransigent of terrorists.

"Wolf 3, Wolf 4 to strike leader. We're catching up the wigglers and squirters."

Below, at their three o'clock, two speeding half-tracks made a fast break for the shelter of the wadi, (dried-up creek bed) that had once been the freshwater source for the Crusader fort. A dozen enemy soldiers in each vehicle sprayed a withering hail of AK-47 rounds toward the pursuing HAWGS, peppering their armored cockpits and fuel tanks to no avail. With the reputation of virtual indestructibility, they demonstrated why they are known as Tank Killers by pulling behind the two vehicles and ripping them with 30mm cannon fire. The rolling fireballs spewed out a hand-full of men running for their lives. A second pass rolled them up like a twelve-gauge Mossberg shotgun rolling a country briar patch rabbit. Done and done!

Strike Leader Rooster miked back, "Roger, Wolf 3, Wolf 4, EA-6B standing your twelve o'clock for another five. Chew some ass."

On the other side of the battlefield Wolf 2 miked to Wolf 1. "Hard right. Launcher on your six."

Turning hard in his seat and looking over his left shoulder, Wolf 1 could see four enemy soldiers emerge from a hidden bunker shouldering SAMs with his name on them! Wolf 1 yanked the stick hard left while simultaneously kicking the rudder full left with his boot. As Wolf 1 made his feinting juke move, Wolf Two rolled out of the tail end of the figure eight, howling out of the dust cloud surrounding the compound. Wolf 2 let loose his hungry 30s, BUZZZZZ, BUZZZZZZZ, BUZZZZZZZZ. The four terrorists vaporized in puffs of pink smoke.

The four A-10s counted off, "Wolf 1 clear, Wolf 2 clear, Wolf 3 clear, Wolf 4 clear."

Wolf 1 to strike leader, "Rallying to Mother Jugs for a quick teat, then outbound."

"Roger, Wolf 1. Safe ride guys. Good job."

A SEAL Team member surveying the aftermath of Operation Conundrum turned to Master Chief Rawlings.

"Sir, for a bunch of jarheads, they sure put a fuckin' on those rat bastards down there, didn't they, sir?"

Rawlings ground his jaws and shot a disgusting stream of tobacco spittle in the direction of the compound.

"He's still a washout!"

Of the thousand terrorists in General Ahmed Ibrahim's army, only one survived. Crawling from a smoking pile of twisted steel and concrete rubble, a bloodied and torn fighter was the sole survivor, quickly identified electronically as Kamal Rashid. His left knee ripped by shrapnel and his left eye blinded, he shook his fist at the receding sound of after burners and cursed The Great Satan. Vowing revenge by the Sword of Allah, he would carry the crippling mark of the Infidels for life.

At the CIC on the Nimitz, all carrier-based strike assets returned safely. The A-10s reported safely routed to a friendly airfield. The Vice-Admiral Battle Group Commander convened his staff to review an After-Action Report compiled by the SEALS on the ground, confirming all hardened targets and armored assets were destroyed. General Ibrahim and his command staff were all killed. The Battle Group Commander adjusted his reading glasses, folded the report, and tossed it onto his desk.

Looking up to the CAG, he voiced unusual praise. "God bless those HAWGS. Those two imbedded Saudi traitors damn near screwed our pooch. We bring 'em in, train 'em knowing most of 'em hate us and all we represent. Then we're supposed to be surprised when they turn on us. It's all political bullshit. Any survivors on the ground?"

"One Sir. A raggedy ass nobody going by the name of Kamal Rashid was secreted away disguised as a local Bedouin. Reportedly, he was shot up pretty bad. Probably lying dead somewhere in the desert."

"Very well. Dog it off and copy the United States Consulate. They'll brief the Saudis."

CHAPTER 3: KAMAL

K amal Rashid's jihad with the West began with the Soviet attack on Afghanistan in 1979. With his village laid waste, Kamal lay hidden and trembling beneath the carcass of a slaughtered sheep as his Saudi born Mujahidin father and two older brothers were executed by the Russians. He watched his mother being raped and garroted by a dozen Russian soldiers drunk on adrenaline and blood lust. Her last act in this life was to enclose a religious amulet into her son's hands as she hid him away. That was the day young and innocent Kamal Rashid lost his soul to the dark side, lost his soul to Satan. Matured and battle hardened by age 14, Kamal was pulled into worldwide Jihad by the gravitational messianic power of Osama bin Laden. His empty and aimless soul drank from bin Laden's rhetoric, soaking his bones in it, just as dry sand soaks up water, fueling his rage and pain, offering him a target to which he could direct his anger.

Loyal as he was ruthless in pursuit of his master's visions, Kamal moved quickly up the ranks of the Al Qaeda insurgency. Groomed to become one of Osama's top lieutenants, Kamal was provided a clean identity and sent by way of distant relatives to America for his education. Kamal would live in two worlds, inwardly burning the hot fires of jihad, while outwardly seeming to be the perfect transfer student with a travel visa that opened America's doors to his vindictive mind.

Boston College gave Kamal a degree in mechanical engineering. The city's proximity to the Canadian border allowed casual day trips across the border, which he used to build relationships with the growing Muslim population in Toronto. There Kamal planted the seeds of jihad into sleeper cells of true believers, biding their time waiting for commands from Osama, yearning for the sweet afterlife of martyrdom.

In 2006 Kamal narrowly missed getting swept up in the dragnet capture of the Toronto 18, an Al Qaeda splinter group. They were accused of planning to detonate truck bombs, open fire in crowded areas, and storm the Canadian Broadcasting Centre, the Canadian Parliament Building, and Canadian Security Intelligence Service. They also prepared to take hostages and behead the Prime Minister and other leaders. Kamal was the unseen, faceless man behind the curtain.

Kamal freely used his student travel visa to reconnoiter potential targets in Canada and the US. A secret Islamist smuggling ring operating in the St. Lawrence Seaway gave him unfettered international access and regular trips back to Afghanistan. Kamal's fluency in English, French, and Farsi safely navigated him back and forth from the Great Satan to his homeland. He was keenly aware that United States and

Canadian Customs were hard pressed to inspect 2% of all the cargo traveling the seaway into Canada. It was an opportunity waiting for its chance.

Unlimited in his scope of hatred for the West, Kamal Rashid sought every opportunity to exact his vengeance. Using his Saudi birthright, Rashid became a double agent and a junior officer in the Saudi National Army, outwardly supporting the Saudi regime. His true Master, however, was Osama Bin Laden. Rashid took advantage of dual allegiances to secretly support a rogue Saudi General's plan to overthrow the Saudi regime as punishment for its support of the Western power's opposition to the spread of Sharia law and world-wide jihad.

The great plot exposed by American intelligence died in a pile of desert rubble, unknown, unmarked, and buried in international ambiguity.

When America's SEAL Team Six killed his mentor, Osama bin Laden, May 2, 2011, Kamal Rashid became unhinged. His rage knew no bounds. He plotted and planned. He carried out several public beheadings of captured westerners to feel their throats beneath his knife. Their hot red blood was his orgasm of radical jihad.

Boston kept running through Rashid's mind. Allah was giving him a sign; Take your vengeance in Boston!

For months Kamal Rashid planned a series of suicide bombings that would drive a stake through the heart of the Great Satan. They would instill a fear so great in American's lives that they would see jihad behind every bush, in every strange vehicle in the park, or across the street from their homes. His revenge would be on a grand scale, six bombings on the same day, beginning with the date of Patriots Day, 2013.

Kamal recruited six sets of volunteers to martyr themselves, delivering suicide bombs to detonate simultaneously at the finish line of the 2013 race, at Boston College, City Hall, a railroad tunnel, a Veteran's Hospital, and Logan International Airport.

Despite all his care and planning, it was impossible to completely hide the massive communication network required to pull off an attack as coordinated as this. The FBI and Homeland Security had noticed some of the chatter and divined that something big was in the works. One of the names that kept popping up... Kamal.

Senior FBI analyst and former field agent Dan Shields was the invisible spook in Kamal's rear-view mirror. Tracking leads, squeezing informants, and using detective algorithms, Shields and his team slowly began to put some of the pieces together, like a child's connect-a-dot picture. Each speck of information added to the picture, slowly coming into focus.

Suspicious internet activity and informants placed in mosques netted most of the plotters before they could carry off the attack. All but two were either jailed on suspicion of plotting terrorist activities or became scared and faded back into the Muslim community.

The two Tsarnaev brothers, Tamarin fresh from the training camp in Pakistan, and the younger Dzhokhar firmly in his older brother's control, remained outside Agent Shield's radar screen. The older brother had fallen through the cracks of the terror watch list process, the younger an invisible tag-a-long.

A frustrated Kamal Rashid was determined to conduct his plan to the last man, inspiring the two brothers to place their pressure cooker bombs in knapsacks along the finish line of the Boston Marathon. He encouraged them to be true to The Word, reciting a bin Laden fatwa:

"The ruling to kill Americans and their allies, civilian and military, is an individual duty for every Muslim who can do it in any country in which it is possible to do it. This is in accordance with the words of Almighty God who said to fight the pagans all together as they fight you all together and fight them until there is no more tumult or oppression, and there prevail justice and faith in God."

Kamal would watch from a safe rooftop one block away, his hand on a remote detonator should his accomplices' nerves fail them.

The rest is history, played out on the news around the world. The police and FBI dragnet surrounding Boston soon ran to ground and killed the older Tamerlan Tsarnaev. Several days later, Dzhokhar was captured. Kamal had long since vanished into the jihadist underworld, invisible, but not yet free. Kamal's sixth sense instinct of a hunted animal could "feel" the dogged footsteps of Dan Shield's task force closing in on him. Fearing a trap at the border, Kamal did the last thing the FBI's most decorated terrorist hunter thought he would do. He turned away from the Canadian border, shaved his beard and donned the flashiest tourist rags he could find. Sporting heavily shaded sunglasses and a corrective prosthetic shoe to hide his crippled gate, Kamal Rashid became forensically invisible, hiding in plain sight.

CHAPTER 4: YELLOWSTONE

K amal Rashid was hiding in plain sight, disguised as a tourist on a Tauk Tour bus making a four-week tour across the western United States. His plan was to lie low, go with the flow, and jump the tour bus at his earliest opportunity. He would make the overnight hike across the Canadian border to safety and be picked up by a fellow Muslim contact from a cell out of Toronto. The next-to-last stop on the tour itinerary was Yellowstone National Park.

The tour started with a twenty-five-minute film on the history of the park and its geology, presented by resident park geologist Dr. George Ainslee.

"Yellowstone National Park has a history as old as America itself. Native Americans called Yellowstone home as far back as eleven thousand years ago. Home to both the Kiowa and Crow tribes, it was a sacred place, alive, beautiful, and cruel. Both Indian tribes shared a common ancestral creation story about the nature of Yellowstone's hot springs and thermals. One, called The Dragon's Mouth for its cavernous "mouth" spewing hot breath, steam and sulfur fumes was, according to legend, the hand of the Creator who gave them Yellowstone for their home. Yellowstone's name comes from the yellow color of sandstone cliffs you can still see today along the lower Yellowstone River.

"European traders and fur trappers first came into this area in the early 1700s looking for Native Americans to trade with. The famed Lewis and Clarke Expedition of 1803-04 never saw Yellowstone, instead navigating around its perimeter on their way to the west coast. The War of 1812 slowed white exploration of Yellowstone for several years, after which famous names such as Jim Bridger began publicizing the areas many natural wonders.

"Yellowstone National Park was first established in 1872. Its boundaries have been enlarged several times since, currently covering 3,472 square miles, larger than the states of Delaware and Rhode Island combined. The Park spreads across the three states of Wyoming, Montana, and Idaho, hosting millions of visitors each year. Yellowstone is an active volcanic system. It experiences three-thousand small earthquakes annually, has ten-thousand hydrothermal features, and three hundred geysers; the most famous one is, of course, Old Faithful. We have two hundred ninety waterfalls, one being the tallest in the continental United States, at three hundred and eight feet tall. The Park proudly hosts every species of bird, mammal, and plant system surviving since the discovery of America. And most notably, Yellowstone contains the largest volcanic caldera in the world, measuring forty-five by thirty miles.

"You, ladies and gentlemen, are sitting on top of the largest bucket of boiling, molten lava on Planet Earth, just five miles below your seats. Yellowstone's super volcano status is earned by its unequaled history of volcanic eruptions of almost unimaginable proportions. Yellowstone has had a major eruption about every six hundred thousand years, the first 2.1 one million years ago, the second, 1.3 three million years ago, and the last 640 thousand years ago. Geologically, we are overdue for another one. Hawaii's Kilauea volcano is a mere squirt gun compared to Yellowstone."

Kamal became lost in his thoughts, physically squirming and chafing at this boring drivel, his mind's eye visualizing the Canadian border and safety from the American pursuit that was surely on his tail.

Dr. Ainslee's film persona directed any questions to his assistant, Dr. Christy Albright, who walked out onto the stage.

"Good morning and welcome to Yellowstone. I'm sure you have some questions following Dr. Ainslee's presentation."

"Yes, there in the third row."

"Dr. Ainslee said Yellowstone is overdue for another eruption. What would that look like, and how would that affect America today?"

Kamal snapped back to the present, some black instinct smelling opportunity.

"Well, Ma'am, I wouldn't lose any sleep over it. Geological time ticks by in millennia, not human time. The next eruption if it happens, could be tomorrow, or ten thousand years from now. The Park geologists are constantly monitoring every aspect of the volcano. We would know when something started to happen."

"Yes, you up there in the back." Dr. Albright pointed to a more intuitive young person.

"But what would happen if Yellowstone did erupt, really?"

"If Yellowstone does erupt, and if it mimics the last eruption, the outcome would be catastrophic for North America. The last eruption blew a hole in the earth, ejecting two hundred forty cubic miles of real estate into the atmosphere. That's enough material to bury Texas five feet deep. It rained ash and cinders a foot deep for a thousand miles in every direction, killing herds of prehistoric rhinoceros, camels, and other animals. The blast was twenty-five hundred times the strength of the Mt. St. Helena event of 1980. Such an event today would kill every human being within a thousand-mile radius with a life smothering layer of ash. Chicago would experience a nuclear like black out. A medieval darkness would descend upon the land, crops would die, livestock would suffocate, and millions of North Americans would die, their lungs shredded by inhaling abrasive volcanic ash. The event would dust the East coast with several inches of ash. Power grids would collapse. In short, the United States of America and Canada would go dark. It would be an apocalyptic event."

"That, that can't really happen, can it?" gasped a terrified mother of three.

"Not likely. It would take some sort of impact event of tremendous power, or a seismic shift, or fracture of a geologic fault line under the park to spark a sudden, unexpected eruption such as I describe. It's not likely to happen, even in your grandchildren's lifetimes."

"Thank you for your attention, and if there are no more questions, please enter the park and enjoy your visit to Yellowstone."

Kamal Rashid's seat was empty. He had an epiphany and awakened to a great new plan.

CHAPTER 5: SPOOKS

Boston based FBI Senior Analyst Dan Shields was getting more pissed with every new revelation of poor investigation! His Knob Hill accent raked the room with acerbic bluntness.

"I want to know how we missed this one. Field agents interviewed that Tsarnaev kid two times last year, and still he never made it onto the watch list. We reviewed his passport, we knew where he had traveled and for how long, but sorry, no exact details. Well, shit! He sure as hell didn't go to Pakistan to Boy Scout Camp."

The assembled group of FBI, CIA, and Homeland Security officers reviewing the After-Action Report following the Boston Marathon bombing was not used to being "taken to the woodshed" in such a direct and uncompromising manner.

"We found out about his mother's jihadist sympathies, and we did nothing. Freedom of speech, my ass! This shit has got to stop! And now we got a line on this will-o'-the-wisp Kamal character. How does an obviously Middle Eastern looking guy with one blind eye and a heavy limp walk right past us when we are supposed to be looking for an on the run Middle Eastern looking guy with a blind eye and heavy limp? That shit won't wash with me!" The emotion in his fierce green eyes transfixed everyone in the room, leaving no doubts about his determination to catch the cowardly bastard.

A hand in the third row raised. "Sir!"

"Hold that thought. I'll get to you in a minute."

Dan was just getting wound up. "No stop and search, that's how! We don't want to hurt anyone's FEELINGS. This whole investigation has been a cluster fuck from day one."

Growing up hard in an Irish family of seven children groomed a personality in Dan Shields that saw the world in sharply contrasting shades of black and white. That fuzzy gray line between them was for politicians and whiners. The FBI Academy found a perfect pupil in Dan Shields. Duty was more than a job; it was a calling. He did his job well, earning a reputation which spoke loudly on the wall of Honor at the bureau office in Boston. But it hung like an ill-fitting suit on those with more polished political ambitions. Despite being a little too hard around the edges for top management, his relentless pursuits and dogged results could not be overlooked.

Aged 38, a student of martial arts, a past Top Shot on the FBI shooting team and fit as an oak timber, agent Dan Shields worked his way up the FBI ladder to Senior Analyst of domestic terrorism. His prematurely gray temples pulsed with the passionate demands of his job. His quick, green eyes missed nothing, and there was no quit in him when it came to solving cases.

"This Kamal guy is bad news. Everywhere he goes, he leaves a trail of bodies behind him. And now he's vanished. Shit! You all know he's not done yet. I want you to tap any line you need to; squeeze any informant, shake down every low life who even smells funny. And get hold of my counterpart in the Canadian Security Intelligence Service. I want to put a squeeze play on our man. I don't think he made it out of the country from any major airport. We shut down a quick escape north of Boston into Canada. This guy is smart enough to see what we don't. If we shake enough trees, something will fall out. Somebody knows this guy. We're going to do whatever it takes to catch him."

The forgotten third row guy interrupted again. "Agent Shields, sir. Are you asking us to break the rules?"

"Son, didn't you hear me the first time? We are going to do whatever it takes. You see any wiggle room in that statement? You can hang all this on me if it gets sideways. In this day and time, with every radicalized Tom, Dick, and Hussein looking to cut off our heads, I'd rather get my pink slip than a toe tag.

"Any more questions?

"Gentlemen, the FBI Counterintelligence and Counter Terrorism budget is $3.1 billion. Let's try to give the American people their monies worth on this one. Get cracking."

One week later, a tip about a missing tourist made its way onto Dan Shield's desk. Agent Shields followed the lead with a phone call to the Tauk Tour company out of Boston, Massachusetts.

"You got a name for this guy?"

"He booked his trip in the name of Al-Khadir."

"Yes, Sir," replied the dispatcher on duty. "One of our tour buses has reported that a passenger disappeared from a tour to Yellowstone National Park last week. He paid for his four-week western tour in cash and carried little luggage. And he was dark complexioned, possibly of Middle Eastern origin."

Agent Shields, sensing a possible crack in the case, doodled a note on his scratch pad. "This guy fits the profile."

"Yep, got it. Go on."

"Our driver reported that this passenger kept to himself when the tour started in Boston. He sat alone, ate alone, and bunked alone. He was noticed missing when the tour bus left Yellowstone for the return trip routing through the Southwestern United States."

"Is there anything else?"

"No sir, that's all we know. Well, maybe. I don't know if this helps, the driver did notice the guy always wore dark shades and had a slight limp."

"Can you fax the manifest for that tour to my office?"

"Yes, sir. Bringing it up now. It's on the way."

"Thank you very much. You've been most helpful."

Hanging up the phone and snatching the tour manifest from the fax machine, Dan Shields turned to his assistant. "Book my flight to Wyoming. I'm going to follow up on this one personally. And run a make on the name Al-Khadir. Call me as soon as you get something."

Upon touch down at the Jackson Hole Airport, a Park Ranger met Shields and dropped him at the Park Research Center where he was met immediately at the front door.

"Welcome to Yellowstone, Agent Shields. I'm Dr. George Ainslee, Director of Geologic Studies at Yellowstone. Your Boston office gave us a heads up that you were coming. Let's go upstairs. I'll introduce you to my assistant, Dr. Christy Albright."

They stepped out of the elevator into a heated discussion.

"Dammit, Dr. Albright. My guys are drilling just where you told us to drill. You treat that thing like it's your child. Well, your baby just swallowed another section of drill tube. That's three in two days, at a cost of nearly $10,000 in labor and material each time! They're dropping off into a great nothing down there. Why can't you pick a better place for your bore holes?" He waived a sheaf of papers to add emphasis to his complaint.

Dr. Albright squared off to face the driller. "To get the precise readings I need, means you have to drill exactly where I tell you to drill. My baby is talking, and I need those test sites to understand what she's saying. Am I making myself clear?"

"Yes, Ma'am, perfectly clear."

Mumbling to himself, the flustered engineer shook his head and turned to leave, knowing he was not going to win this one. Half-way out the door he turned to Dan Shields with a look that said, "Good luck, buddy."

Dr. George Ainsley turned toward his assistant, directing her attention to their guest.

"Dr. Albright, I want you to meet our guest from the FBI. Agent Dan Shields, meet Dr. Christy Albright."

Where Dr. Ainslee's earlier handshake had been neither firm nor slack, just a reflexive gesture, Christy Albright's was surprisingly crisp, affirmative, and direct as the steady gaze of her piercing blue eyes. Framed by a cap of rusty red hair, tall and fit, she was self-assured in her manner.

"Agent Shields, how may we help you?"

"I'm here to follow up on a lead about a suspect I've been tracking. He may have been here within the last week, hiding in a tour group visiting the park. Can you show me the same presentation he would have seen?"

"Sure thing. Let's start with a tour of our research center, then we'll show you the Welcome to Yellowstone orientation film our tour groups see.

"Doctor Albrig—"

"Call me Christie if I can call you Dan. Our work around here is technical enough without having to call each other by our professional names."

"Good enough." Dan took an immediate interest in the Geologist with the hard cover and soft edges.

"Your study of Yellowstone's tectonic history and the procedures you used to monitor the volcano are actually quite similar to my work at the Bureau. Both are forensic exercises. The only difference being that you're trying to explain what will happen in the future, while I'm chasing the past."

Christie pondered the instant analysis for a second.

"I have the manifest here for the people on the tour I'm inquiring about. My people tried to put names to faces. I know it's a long shot, would you look at these photos to see if you remember anything odd about them?"

"You're telling me you're chasing somebody, and you don't even know what he looks like?"

"The Bureau knows extraordinarily little about this guy. Some ugly history, some sketchy TOP SECRET business in the desert a while back; nothing I can share with you here. No actual photograph, he's a real shady dude.

Abruptly feeling the need to adjust her perception of the resources of the FBI, Christie formulated a plan. "How about we grab lunch at the Cowboy Bar & Grill and talk it over? It's well past lunch time in Boston."

"Sounds good. That airplane food tastes like cardboard."

Christie offered, "I'll drive," pointing to her Jeep Cherokee parked just outside her office window.

A few minutes later Shields could smell the aroma of something savory cooking on a wood-burning grill. His stomach growled in response.

The double-sided swing doors of the Cowboy Bar & Grill resembled those in the long running TV show "Gunsmoke" Longbranch Saloon. They opened to a comfortably upbeat atmosphere filled with the smell of mountain pine, leather, and beer. Bar seats topped with real horse saddles stretched one hundred feet facing a time-stained oak bar backed by twelve-foot mirrors reaching to the ceiling. Two bar tenders in white aprons, white shirts, and sleeve garters were steadily shoveling favorite food and libations to their patrons. Several Jackson locals hunkered over pool tables across from the bar; their beers, cigarettes, and side bet money balanced on the green clothed rub rails. Several tourist types in big city clothes, trying to blend in with the local scene, stood out like a three-legged cow in a rodeo.

An old gray dog in the corner by the cast iron wood-burning stove stoically surveyed it all with one sleepy eye, yawned, and didn't give a damn.

Christie motioned to a table in a back corner, comfortable for a quiet conversation. Dan Shields moved to pull her chair for her. She quipped, "A lady doesn't see that in this place very often."

The two made small talk while they settled in, each reviewing the menu.

"Doctor, I mean Christie, I'm having what you're having."

Christie grabbed a passing waitress by the arm. "Amy, two Cowboy Burgers, trashed, with an order of Buffalo chips on the side."

Dan got right to it, briefing Christie on the reason he was looking for Kamel Rashid. "Right now, catching this Kamel character is my top priority." Dan planted both hands smartly, palms down, on the table for emphasis.

Christie noticed, "I see you aren't wearing a ring. Your life, your wife?"

"The Bureau is my life right now. Not much time for a social life. You know, too many bad guys to catch, and they don't work nine to five. How about you? You really raked that engineer over the coals back there at your office."

"He has his job, I have mine."

Changing the subject because he felt an instant attraction to this fiery red head, Shields asked, "Listen, I noticed several security cameras at the entrance to your office compound. Got anything like that in the tourist theater? Do your security people tape those presentations?"

"I believe they do, on a rolling weekly basis. I mean, they can review any incident that may occur. The tapes automatically record over the prior week's tape unless there's a reason to preserve them."

"Humor me. Let's take a long shot here. Can we get your tech guys to roll this past week's tape on the chance my suspect was on one of those tours?"

Dan wiped off the last of his Cowboy Burger with a napkin and motioned over to Amy to cash out, leaving a $20 tip.

Christie flashed Dan a smile with a slight toss of her fiery red hair. "Big spender for a By-the-book G-Man. Amy will appreciate your kindness."

Slightly flushed, Dan stepped behind Christie to slide her chair back from the table. As Christy rose and turned to leave the table, her hand lightly brushed Dan's hand on the chair. She caught a whiff of his aftershave. They both felt it, like the static shock from a wintertime doorknob. Neither said a word, each knowing however that something passed between them.

At the compound ten quiet minutes later, Christie and Dan spent the balance of the afternoon reviewing Dan's files and running a film clip of the canned tourist presentation. They both seemed to like the closeness of sharing a single monitor.

"Nothing new here," quipped Dan. "Where's that tech guy?"

Christie called him up on the office intercom. "Howard, could you please roll the live guest film from last week's orientation?"

"All of them?"

"Hold a second, Howard."

"Dan, you told me the tour group in question confirmed a missing passenger, right? What day was that."

Dan quickly ran through his notes.

"That'd be last Wednesday."

"Howard, roll Wednesday."

"Rolling in 5, Doctor Albright."

The footage revealed nothing of interest until just before the end of Christie's presentation. One man rose from his seat and exited the rear of the theatre. His face offered only a side profile, but his stride was telling. He had a discernable limp.

"Gotcha!" exclaimed Dan.

"Christie, I'm going to need that footage. My guys may be able to wring a little more detail from those images. We have some fantastic new software back at the Bureau called Rekognition, just developed by Amazon. It can do wonders with iffy images like this one. At least now I know the ghost I've been chasing has a weakness. I can profile that limp."

Dan's cell phone rang as he prepared to stand. "Dan, that name you asked about, al-Khadir, is a reference to an ancient Arabic prophet called the 'The Green One', or 'The Verdant One' and the address he gave was bogus, too."

"Thank you, Cyndi, you're right on time."

Turning to Christie, Dan shook his head with a smile. "Karma's a bitch. That tourist with a limp traveling under the name of al-Khadir is the same guy on this video, also with a limp. Kamil Rashid and al-Khadir are one and the same. I'll be damned. And the bastard thinks himself some kind of prophet."

Christie called up to the projection room. "Howard, could you please bring that tape down to Agent Shields?"

"On the way."

As Dan prepared to leave the Yellowstone research center, he turned to Dr. Ainslee.

"Nice meeting you, Doc. As much as I'd like to stay to see more of this beautiful place, I'll be on first plane out of here in the morning."

"Perhaps another time then," Ainslee replied. "Hope we've been of some help."

Turning to Christie, he extended his hand. "Here's my card. My personal cell number is on the back. Call me anytime, 24/7, especially if something new comes to mind, will you?"

As Dan Shields made his goodbyes, Dr. Ainslee thought to himself, "Seems like a decent enough guy. I was expecting a steely-eyed hard ass."

Christie mumbled something to herself as the door closed behind the departing FBI agent. He had a little extra snap to his stride, but he also seemed a bit reluctant to leave.

Christie put Dan's card in her lab coat pocket, then pulled it out again, turning it over to the phone number on the back. For a second, her mind turned to more than science. "He's staying overnight. Should I, or not?" The thought passed quickly, and she put the card back into the pocket of her lab coat.

Preparing for an early morning flight out of Jackson, Agent Shields looked out a side window of his plane and cursed himself, "Dammit man, what's wrong with you?"

Quickly turning in his seat toward a stewardess preparing for her routine departure safety lecture, Dan flashed his FBI badge. "Excuse me, Miss. I need to get off this plane. I'm sorry for the disruption."

Minutes later, after mustering Park Security, a nervous Shields took a deep breath and knocked on Christie's lab door. Almost regretting his decision, he couldn't take it back when the door opened, to Christie's surprise, looking up from her clipboard. About to say something glib, she was hushed by Dan's right index finger to his mouth. He was committed. The words came blurting out, out from a heart long hardened against such emotional vulnerability. He looked her straight in the eyes. "I'm hanging myself out on an unfamiliar limb here, but I can't let the moment go. I have to see you again."

Not quite sure of her own heart, Christie blushed slightly. "But I don't date. We talked about that at lunch, don't you remember?"

Quickly reverting to agent mode, Dan countered. "It's not a date. It's a dinner. Everyone must eat."

Regaining her composure and actually enjoying the tease, she retorted, "I eat only Beef Wellington on Thursday nights. If you can find Beef Wellington by 8pm tonight, I'll dine with you."

Without missing a beat, Dan pulled out his phone and called his office in Boston. "I'm laying over another day. Got a couple more moves to check on."

Both oars back in the water again, Dan closed with, "I'll pick you up at eight."

"You don't know where I live."

He smiled a boyish smile as he turned to leave. "Hey, I'm the FBI."

As she closed the door Christie mused. "This is a cowboy town. Not a Beef Wellington within 200 miles."

Twelve hours is a long time chasing something that cannot be found. Dan discovered that truth after being turned away by every restaurant in Jackson. "Beef Wellington is a multi-layered meal taking all day to prepare, and certainly not for a single meal."

Five o'clock arrived, and sweating over his 8pm deadline, Dan was running out of options when an idea hit him. He made a couple of secure calls.

"Hook me up with the next high dollar private party jetting into Jackson. Tell 'em the FBI needs a favor. It will not be forgotten."

By seven-forty-five Christie was thoughtfully swirling her normal after work glass of wine, recalling Dan's surprise knock on her door. "No way this guy can pull it off. But he was cute. And he did really put it all out there. The guy's got balls for sure. I'll throw on something casual, just in case. Worst-case scenario, I can bop down to the Cowboy Bar & Grill for a nightcap and some good music."

The doorbell sounded. Christie looked up at the clock, ticking the last few seconds before eight.

"No way."

She opened the front door to find Dan Shields dressed in a full tuxedo, carrying a covered dish on a silver service tray in his left hand and a bottle of champagne in his right.

Without a word, Dan bowed slightly, and seizing the initiative, stepped through the doorway, setting the tray and bottle of champagne on a side table. Going for broke, he then pulled a speechless Christie Albright into his embrace with a long deep kiss that left her knees wobbly.

The next morning Christy rolled over in her empty bed and started upright with the overhead passing of the 6:45 flight out of Jackson. "O my God. This was a mistake." Gasping for breath, she saw a hand-written letter where her lover had lain. The lengthy letter recounted breathless confessions shared in the night, about lives loved and lost, and closed with, "Selflessly in your service, Dan."

Christie collapsed back onto the bed, her head spinning.

The two new lovers swapped e-letters and phone calls over the next few weeks.

"When can I see you again, Dan?"

"I've got some R & R coming. How about I fly in and whisk you off to a private little island off Nantucket for a week of surf, sun, and lobster? We'll fish, walk the beach, and take sunset cruises. We'll step off life's racetrack, off the grid. I need a break from the fast pace at the Bureau and there is no one on the planet I'd rather share it with than you."

"You're on. And Dan, this time I'll bring the Beef Wellington."

Dan about fell out laughing over the phone. "And I'll bring the dessert."

Fate had other plans.

Eight weeks after Kamal made his break from the Yellowstone tour, a falsely registered freighter departed from Canada by way of the St. Lawrence Seaway and made port at the Red Sea terminal of Karachi, Pakistan. Two days later Kamal Rashid met with his Al Qaeda brothers.

A new day had come for jihad!

CHAPTER 6: CAIN AND ABEL

A summer solstice full moon bathed the California seaside bar in a pale-yellow glow. The high tide surf pounding the beach lent a subtle background beat to the hot dance music ebbing from beneath the palm thatched roof. Drink napkins and lady's skirts danced gently in the warm, salty ocean breeze. It was two years prior to the 2013 Boston Marathon bombing.

Raptors Bar & Grill was a local bar in the military town of Coronado, California. Just a stone's throw from the ocean, the laid-back atmosphere was welcome relief from the mental and physical grind of military life. The driftwood paneled walls embraced the semicircular bar, a clear poly top was embedded with local seashells and offered buckets of salty roasted peanuts begging for cool libation. Free spinning bar stools gave a 360-degree access to any conversation or pretty face. A steady onshore breeze cooled the place. The walls and ceiling were decorated with thousands of stapled one dollar bills that generations of patrons left as testimony to their passage through Raptors Bar & Grill. A cold brew, good music, and occasional dance with a pretty girl could ease almost any pain from the rigors of military training. Fifty cents bought five favorite tunes from the 1960s era juke box in the corner.

Ensign AC Collins turned to his newfound drinking buddy and downed another shot of Fireball. "Toad, this is a target rich environment my friend."

Both men having just met at a new duty station were each out on the town for one last blowout party before entering the United States Navy SEAL training program the next day. Destiny seemed to have sought them out from opposite ends of the social spectrum, bringing each man to this point in his military career for a future neither could ever have anticipated.

The rusty red and chrome trimmed juke box clunked and fetched John C. Fogerty's prescient tune, "Bad Moon Rising."

As the needle hit the vinyl Ronnie Toad Rawlings nodded in agreement, saluted the juke box, and knocked back a third shot of his favorite hooch.

---"I see a bad moon a-risin',
I see trouble on the way,
I see earthquakes and lighting,
I see bad times today" ---

AC challenged Toad. "You got no game with the ladies."

---"Don't go around tonight
It's bound to take your life,
There's a bad moon on the rise"

"Says you."

Training his one sober eye on a gorgeous red-haired lady across the room, Toad began his target run. His drunken tunnel vision dismissed the two Marines who had the girl boxed in against the jukebox, but not her obvious attempt to get rid of them.

One Marine asked, "Hey baby, want to take a walk with a real man?" He grabbed her left hand and pressed it to his crotch. "Smoke this."

Before Toad could close to within striking distance, one of the Marines grabbed the girl roughly by the arm, saying something Toad couldn't understand. He did understand the gist of it when she slapped the smirk from the face of her unwelcome suitor.

> ---"I hear hurricanes a-blowing
> I know the end is coming soon,
> I fear the rivers overflowing,
> I hear the voice of rage and ruin" ---

The ruffian raised his hand in reply, and all hell broke loose.

> ---"Hope you got your things together
> Hope you are quite prepared to die.
> Looks like we're in for nasty weather,
> One eye is taken for an eye" ---

Mission aborted.

Alerted by the loud SMACK, patrons scattered as Toad closed with the two men. Toad hooked the first man's raised right arm with his own and leveraging his own

70

weight and strength with a hip roll and a single leg takedown, slammed the Marine flat on his back. The red head shrieked and ran behind the bar, huddling with the bartender who was on the phone calling the Military Police. As Toad regained his feet, the second Marine broke a wooden bar stool across his back, knocking him to the floor. Before the man could take advantage of the moment, AC, having watched all this unfold in a skinny two or three seconds, picked up a busted chair leg and began beating the hell out of the second Marine.

The bar emptied into the parking lot, sirens wailing and blue lights dancing off an iridescent sea fog.

Toad regained his feet and nodded a bloodied "thanks" to AC, giving the groaning Marine on the floor a parting kick in the ribs.

"Stupid jarhead."

---"Don't go around tonight
Well, it's bound to take your life,
There's a bad moon on the rise" ---

Toad and AC both turned to the bar, and pulling the red head in tow, bolted for the back door.

"We gotta haul ass."

Out on the beach they ran a few hundred yards downwind of the barstool mayhem to the safety of a sand dune ridge out of sight of the bar, and the MP's flashing blue lights. The foaming surf soaked them to the waist.

A trailing tune on the swirling ocean breeze faded into the distance,

---"There's a bad moon on the rise." ---

The girl, in a semi-state of shock, finally spoke. "Who the hell are you guys, and why'd you drag me out here?"

"We're gonna be Navy SEALS. My friends call me AC."

"I'm Toad. Looked like you needed some help back there, though I never heard a smack quiet like that one."

"I can take care of myself, thank you. Busting up the place, knocking out two guys, and that's what you call help?"

"What do you call it, AC?"

AC, fixated and staring at Christie's water-soaked tee shirt and cold erect nipples, mumbled, "collateral damage."

"Well, I'm stuck out here cold and wet with a couple of guys named for a battery and a frog."

"You needed saving, and we saved you. That drunken Marine back there didn't look the type to take "No" for an answer. So, what's your name?"

"Christie, Christie Albright."

Toad followed AC's hypnotic gaze and mumbled, "My name is—"

"Yeah, I got it already. Battery man and a wannabe Navy SEAL frogman named Toad. Toad? Your mama couldn't do any better than that?

"That's Ronald Theodocious Rawlings, Ma'am."

AC broke away from the entrancing grip of Christie's fulsome wet titties with an exaggerated, "Theodocious?"

Softening her tone just a bit, Christie replied in a smarmy Southern accent laced with amused sarcasm. "My, my, my, I didn't realize I was in such high company. Bless your hearts."

They all shared a good laugh.

Finally, AC Collins offered, "Listen, the MPs are gone by now. How about I give you a lift? Got my Jeep back there in the parking lot. How about you, Toad?"

"I'm in. I bummed a ride from the barracks."

After dropping Christie at her apartment, AC turned to Toad, mocking him. "And that's what you call game?"

The first day of the SEAL Training Program was destined to set the tone of the friendship between AC and Toad.

When they assembled that first day for inspection on the parade ground, which they learned was called the Grinder, they immediately stood out from the crowd. Toad with a busted and swollen lip, and AC with a black eye.

The SEAL instructor barked, "Collins and Rawlings, step forward. From the looks of it, you boys seem to like to mix it up. You might want to save a little of that extracurricular energy. You're gonna need it to survive this program. You are now government property assigned to me. You will not damage government property assigned to me unless I authorize it. Understood?"

"Sir, yes, sir!" they shouted in unison.

At the command, "As you were," AC and Toad rejoined the ranks behind them.

Addressing the full contingent before him, the SEAL instructor continued. "The six-month SEAL training BUD/S program, that's Basic Underwater Demolition for the phonetically challenged among you," he said, cutting a glance toward Toad, "is among the toughest of special operations training of any of the United States military. Eighty percent of you won't make it."

"BUD/S is going to run you, drill you, deprive you of every soft comfort, pushing you to the extreme, beyond what you think you are capable of, and that's just Phase One. If you survive Hell Week and move to Phase Two, you will learn combat diving and swimming skills, weapons, demolitions, small unit tactics, rappelling, hydro-recon, and marksmanship. It will teach you to operate successfully anywhere in the world, under any conditions. In all of this, you will learn the key to survival and success in the harshest of conditions depends upon teamwork, each of you working seamlessly to accomplish together what no man can do alone. Those of you who survive this six-month phase of the program may advance to the final comprehensive training after which you MAY be offered the coveted Navy SEAL Trident insignia on your uniform, honoring all those who came before you."

Swelling with pride and the adrenaline-fueled passion of the moment, the collective group of new recruits shouted a unanimous "HOO-YAH," before gathering themselves before their steely eyed taskmaster.

The ability to compartmentalize physical and mental challenges is key to survival, both in the BUD/S training program and in the real-world assignments to come. Just as successful marathon runners channel their minds to some inner place to conquer the runner's wall, so did AC and Toad create their own inner space, a safe harbor from the stress that breaks lesser men causing them to "ring out" of the training program.

Allen Carter Collins, AC, was born and raised in Boulder, Colorado, grandson of a decorated Marine Corps fighter pilot who flew Wildcats over Guadalcanal against the Japanese in World War Two. A three-sport letterman in high school and back-up quarterback on his college football team developed AC's leadership skills and respect for teamwork. AC's outlook on life was as clear and fresh as John Denver's Rocky Mountain High.

AC grew up a mountain boy, trout fishing pristine lakes and streams and pheasant hunting blue sky farm fields. The JROTC program in high school set AC on course for ROTC and a military career. The day he graduated college, he found himself engaged with a Navy recruiter. There was Marine Corps blood in his veins, but having known mountains and prairies all his life, he could not withstand the lure of the sea.

Now in Coronado, his cool, calculating personality measured the risk/reward balance of every exchange. Foremost for the next six months was to keep Toad's redneck inclinations under check and below the radar screen of their SEAL instructors' retributions.

Standing six feet four inches tall, naturally tanned and with a killer smile the ladies found irresistible, AC Collins became the counterbalance to Toad's "take no prisoners" approach to life.

Built like a fireplug, no neck, barrel chest, nicked and scarred from a love of Saturday night fist fights, Toad was the Ying to AC's Yang. While the military flat top haircut was a concession to duty for AC, it was "styling" for Toad: a bulldog's pride in his spiked collar!

Expectantly named for better things by his mother, Ronald "Ronnie" Theodocius Rawlings, was on the other end of the social spectrum, an Arkansas redneck of the finest breeding. He grew up in an abusive family with a drunken former Marine Corps Gunnery Sergeant for a father, who abandoned him at age 16 after a final, brutal confrontation.

Gunny Rawlings would nightly stumble home drunk from the bar at AMVET and open with tirades against every perceived slight life had dealt him, calling his wife, "whore," and Ronnie, "you little whore's turd." Verbal abuse would escalate to slapping his wife around and pounding on young Ronnie, who became mote and shield for his shattered mother. So often did this occur that Ronnie's nick name at school was coon eye, because of his regularly blackened eyes from fights with his father. When his mother was killed in a one car drunken accident with his father at the wheel, Ronnie Rawlings left home for good. Father and son have never spoken since.

Young Ronnie Rawlings learned early to give no quarter and expect none from an adversary. "You got to knock me out or kill me."

It was Rawlings take no prisoners personality, and his hard-earned reputation as the go-to guy in two years of prior duty assignments in some nasty places that earned him a coveted shot at making the transition to the SEALS.

Toad's best childhood memories were of hunting wild hogs in Arkansas cane thickets and noodling for catfish along brush covered riverbanks. On one hunting camping trip a sixteen-year-old Ronnie Rawlings and his best running buddy, Sammy Joe Johnson, were daylight floating the marshes of the Little Possum River looking for wild hogs.

"Easy on that paddle, Sammy Joe. Sound travels a mile when it's dead quiet. Listen up now. Odd random noises from out in the marsh are normal creek noise, wind in the grass, water gurglin' down the creek bank, or maybe a gator growl. But when you hear the same noise repeat itself from the same direction more than three times, that's likely hogs away off rootin' marsh grass bulbs or freshwater clams."

The boys floated the early morning fog burning off the river into hard daylight when they heard it, a steady crunching and ripping noise up ahead and about a hundred yards off starboard. It sounded like someone shucking corn stalks, "rip, snap, crunch."

"Shsss," Toad hissed, pointing to some open hog rooting on the edge of the bank where the normally head high marsh grass had been ripped, stripped, and ploughed up. "Sammy Joe, ease the paddle into the mud bank and tie us off, real quiet now." Whispering, "We'll ease along that hog trail downwind o' them hogs. Grab the gun and follow me. Wait for the breeze to rustle the grass. You move when I move, stop when I stop."

Sammy Joe nodded and replied, "Affirmative."

Thirty minutes of careful stalking brought the boys to the edge of a patch of grass fairly rooted down by feeding hogs. Toad pointed to his right ear, then to the crunching sounds fifty feet across the opening and held up three fingers. Just barely visible were several hogs' back lines, their heads down feeding.

Toad motioned Sammy Joe to step forward and shoulder his single barrel 410 slug gun for instant action. The slight head wind dropped to nothing. The crunching grew quiet. Big game this close often have a sixth sense that something's not right. Wild hogs have poor eyesight, so unexpected motion and sound are alarming. An errant boot misstep drew a slurpy sucking sound from the ankle-deep marsh mud. Three sets of shaggy pointed ears rose from the grass. Muffled grunts sounded off as the three hogs searched for an intruder. Toad felt a renewed breeze springing from behind. Touching his nose and motioning to Sammy Joe, "Shit, they're gonna smell us. Get ready." No sooner than the whisper left Toad's lips, the three hogs grunted as one and turned toward their back trail. One false step for a confirming sniff of man smell opened one hog's shoulder to Sammy's gun sight.

"Take him."

Bam! The 410-shotgun muzzle blast echoed across the marsh and down the river. The boar hog, thigh high on a grown man and weighing about two hundred fifty pounds, lurched sideways at the impact of the slug.

Dust and mud flew from the inch thick, hard as green oak, cartilage shoulder shield.

"Hit him again, hit him again," hollered Toad.

While adrenaline shook him, Sammy Joe fumbled the breach to eject the spent shell and reload a second round. The big boar, now more pissed off than hurt, turned on his attackers.

Sammy Joe's hurried second round split the hog's ears, creasing his spine, momentarily putting him down. Unhinged, Sammy Joe dropped his remaining two shells into the mud. No ammo and a wounded hog. Not good. Pushed to fight, wild hogs rarely back down.

His rear end crippled from Sammy Joe's second shot, the angry boar still had his fighting wind, two good legs and a foaming set of four-inch cutter tusks. As the boys turned, so, too, turned the wounded boar, facing his tormentors.

"Les' get the hell out a here Toad!" Sammy Joe screamed.

Toad yelled over the noisy foaming snapping tusks growling, "No way! We gotta finish what we started. You stay in front of him. I'll circle to his rear. Shake the gun at him. I'll take him from behind and finish him with my knife."

Two things happened at once. The boar lurched on his two good legs towards a scared white Sammy Joe. Toad straddled the boar from behind, grabbing the boar's right ear with his left hand while attempting to cut its throat with his right knife hand. In an instant the boar, using his powerful shoulders, swung his busted rear end around, knocking Toad's feet from beneath him. The boar landed on top of Toad who encircled the animal with his legs, his left arm around the boar's neck, his right stabbing the boar's ribcage with his 8-inch Buck hunting knife. Sammy Joe screamed. The enraged boar and desperate Toad were rolling in a muddy death match of squealing growls and redneck cussing.

Approaching wrestler's fatigue, his muscles on fire, Toad was about done for. Then the wild animal survival instinct that is in us all morphed through an adrenaline rush into the rage that defies death and injury. With newfound strength and a primal scream, Toad pressed his attack, driving his knife, again and again, drinking deep of the wild boar's life energy, until he heard the boars' death gurgle, a final shudder, then quiet. Toad rolled out from under the huge carcass onto his back, heaving in his muddy and bloody exhaustion. Almost afraid to know, Toad slowly rolled onto his knees, took a deep breath, and slowly stood. Covered in blood, mud, and pig crap, he thought to himself, "Legs? Check. Arms, belly? Check."

Cracking a wide grin, he turned to a speechless Sammy Joe and hollered, "Goddamn, what a ride!"

After that trip, Sammy Joe volunteered, "My hog huntin' days are over. I'll stick to fishing."

The later grown Ronnie Toad Rawlings became loud, brash, impulsive, and possessed a right hook that could send a man to the Promised Land. Toad became a street brawler, a junkyard dog with allegiance to few, though iron clad loyal, once his acceptance was won.

AC Collins entered the Navy for adventure.

Toad Rawlings signed on looking for the next fight.

The buddy system had never been proven stronger than in the military. AC and Toad became tight. AC's description of the towering mountains of home and the trout filled streams he fished, growing up in Colorado, mesmerized Toad, a siren-call to a place about as far removed from his trailer trash upbringing in Arkansas as it was possible to get. The two fantasized about buying a ranch of their own after military service.

Trout fishing for big, speckled browns, and colored rainbows became that special place in their heads that no pain or discomfort could penetrate. At night in their bunks, they described the place as if they could look right outside the barracks window and see it.

"AC, I wonder what a place like that would cost?"

"Toad, we gotta get finished servin' our country before we worry about that."

One particularly tough team building exercise, meant to cause weaker willed trainees to falter and "ring out" on the quitter's bell, was running in circles carrying a heavy log high overhead. All the team members were grimacing under the strain and pain, except for two. AC and Toad both had stupid, detached smiles on their faces, nodding at each other as if they shared a private joke.

The SEAL instructor hollered down from his parade platform, "Team, double time."

The pain and muscle burn became intolerable. Men were moaning and crying under the strain. Two fell out puking, then rang out, unwilling to endure more torture.

"Collins, Rawlings, you two think this is some kinda joke? You got anything you would like to share with your teammates."

"Sir, no, sir."

Toad couldn't suppress an eye roll toward AC.

"Don't you mock me, boy!" shouted the instructor. "You want the entire squad to do another repetition?"

"Sir, no, sir. This squid does not want to do another repetition, sir."

"Then out with it, boy!"

"Sir, it's just that squid Rawlings caught the biggest trout, sir."

"Trout! Trout, my ass. You ladies better think about inviting all of us to your little fishin' trip next time. There is no 'I' in the word 'team'. Do I make myself understood? Team dismissed!"

The heavy log thumped to the ground. Exhausted men crumpled beside it, all except for AC and Toad, who walked off in animated conversation.

"Toad, you sum bitch. You get that instructor pissed off and life will be hell for both of us!"

"Besides, my trout outweighed yours by half a pound!"

The SEAL instructor put a star by two names on his roster with a margin note. "These boys eat pain like Baby eats chocolate." He shook his head, smiled behind dark green sunglasses, and turned back toward the officers' Quonset hut.

Exemplary in every training exercise, AC Collins and Toad Rawlings cruised through BUD/S qualifying them to become Navy SEALS.

Following graduation from BUDS/S, AC and Toad, along with their teammates, participated in several follow-on SEAL training schools.

One was a training exercise involving six teams from six SEAL instructors. The mission was to infiltrate an enemy position, reconnoiter, and if possible, terminate enemy leadership. The enemy position was a high patch of wooded ground surrounded on three sides by open water, half a mile of salt marsh, and a long causeway from the mainland. Each team was free to make up its own plan and had two hours to execute. The team getting closest to mission goal, won.

The last team of the six to make the attempt was led by Rawlings and Collins. All the others had been caught or laser sighted and Kill shot by the instructors.

A loud air horn signaled the starting time. The first sign that Team Six had begun its exercise was a growing plume of grayish, green smoke coming from the far side of the marsh. Heavy smoke, the kind born of firing dank Spanish moss, pine needles, and wet marsh reeds began to lay down a low thick blanket across the open marsh, gradually smothering the enemy's down-wind position. Instructors in elevated spotting positions and cat walks worked their glasses hard but could find no targets.

Peering over his binoculars, one instructor turned to another, "I told you about those two. Collins is always operating outside the box. And Rawlings, well sometimes I think that boy's not wired right."

"Roger that. Tighten up and be ready for anything."

Meanwhile, two SEAL team members slithered under the cover of smoke into a small salt marsh creek. They would ride the outgoing tide hidden beneath a rack of dead marsh grass; the river debris seen every day on every tide change. Other team members, also hidden by the smoke, made random distracting noises from multiple directions.

The SEAL instructor enemies whispered over their intercoms, randomly speculating about what Team number six's strategy might be. Time was getting short at one hour and forty-five minutes into the exercise when the smoke screen over the marsh began to lift on the evening breeze.

The lead instructor picked up his bull horn, fingering the trigger and glancing back and forth at his watch.

"Chief, what time you got?"

He was anxious to wrap this up and get back to that cooler of cold Bud in his hooch. It had been a long day in the field.

"Almost there, Boss. Besides, those guys aren't actually supposed to win. Too many obstacles, too many eyeballs, too little time. This is a training exercise."

The instructor was about to shut down the exercise when, looking at his watch, he coldly realized that a red laser light had him literally by the balls. The prophylactic covered muzzle of Ronnie Toad Rawlings HK MP5N sniper rifle was poking up through the slats of the catwalk to within ten inches of his crotch.

"I respectfully inform you, sir; you're dead, sir."

One of the other instructors turned to a loud expression of "Holy Shit" when he, too, was lit up, a red laser dot on his chest.

Slowly, the camouflaged forms of Toad Rawlings and AC Collins rose from their slimy lair, all dull to the eye but for two gleaming white smiles. They keyed their mikes twice, the signal to their team members, who returned a loud "HOO-YAH" in the gathering darkness.

Back at the SEAL Team instructor hootch that night, team number six's instructor was collecting his winnings from the other five instructors, a five-hundred-dollar pot for the winning team.

The last entry in his training journal beside his top two graduates read, Petty Officer Rawlings – "Heat Seeker." Lt. Collins – "Tactical."

After graduating as the top two on their SEAL Team's final roster, Toad was declared the Honor Man accolade, while AC was awarded Officer-In-Charge. AC and Toad were assigned a routine training stint aboard submarines. They applied their BUD/S training skills to fight and attack enemy positions using scuba diving skills, naval combat tactics, sonar, and radar operations, etc. They spent countless hours underwater on bag using the sea as a blanket to cover their movements from enemy eyes, breaching heavily guarded and hard to reach places anywhere the sea touches. They gathered intelligence, placed explosives to destroy enemy assets, and infiltrated enemy positions near the coastline before fading away into the ocean.

On one training mission, their boat's objective was to worm its way through a convoy of U.S. Navy destroyers undetected. Failing this test under actual combat conditions against the Russians, Koreans, or Chinese could have deadly consequences.

"AC, I don't like it down here. Boat's too crowded and noisier than a beer fart in a tin outhouse. No way we can sneak past all that surface sonar."

"Toad, the Captain may run this boat, but the guy covering our asses is that wormy little Sonar Operator over there. If he can mimic the sonar signatures of the boats hunting us with a matching signal that he sends out, all they hear is white noise. Probably too complicated for an Arkansas brush popper like you to understand. Creating a speed of sound acoustic mismatch causes both sonar waves to cancel each other out, leaving nothing for the enemy to see. Where the two meet is called the null, and we become invisible."

"Pop this, college boy," replied Toad, giving AC the one-finger salute. "Damn nice trick if he can pull it off. Just the same, I'd rather do my fighting on dry ground with a little more elbow room."

AC fired back at his best friend without missing a beat. "Labiodental fricative for 'f', pluck the yew. 1415 Battle of Agincourt. Digitus impudicus."

"What the fffuck," stuttered a linguistically hamstrung Toad.

"Exactly! Look it up."

Life after graduating SEAL Training School and between training trips was a red light/green light mix of partying. The first thing the guys did was show up at Christie Albright's place one night with a case of beer and three pizzas. AC and Toad had both talked about her during their SEAL training in varying what if imaginary scenarios.

Saturday nights at the Raptors Bar & Grill became a regular date for AC, Toad, and Christie; dancing, drinking, taking a break from the more serious demands of life and career. Christie alternately danced with her two beaus: a bumping, hip grinding ode to Billy Ray Cyrus' "Achy

Breaky Heart" with Toad, then AC breaking in with his upright, high hold spin to classics from Fred Astaire. Each man inquisitively whispering soft invitations into her ear, trying to outpoint the other, serious, whimsical, awkward infatuation. Christie felt the heat of passion in their embrace.

Each night ended with a quiet word and separate good-night kiss to her boys, leaving both men, good friends, at emotional odds over their triangular relationship.

For Christie's part, she occasionally mused about a life with each man, career military guys, rugged, exciting. In real life, Christie would have none of it. She treated them as though she were their big sister, and they her little brothers, always chiding them about their girl chasing antics. She had all she could handle going to school, and her short-term future had no room for a serious romance.

Christie knew her guys would end up gallivanting all over the world with the Navy. The three-way relationship would stay comfortably platonic, though both AC and Toad each held a secret fantasy about some distant future relationship with Christie.

And did they party hard. Their last night together was a real stoker. It was also the night Christie broke the news about her new job.

Christie Albright grew up the only daughter of five children to affluent parents on a horse farm outside of Columbia, South Carolina. She learned to ride, hunt, and shoot with her brothers, developing an independent streak a mile wide. She championed a hellion streak bridled by a lifelong bible study that lent temperance to her self-indulgences. She could roll up a running briar patch cottontail with her Beretta 20 gauge or tag a white tail buck at 200 yards across a soybean field with her Daddy's

Winchester .270 as well as any of her brothers. She had a lot of tomboy in her.

Off to school at the Converse College for rich girls, Christie excelled in math and earth sciences. Unlike most of her classmates, she wanted to do more with her life than hunt for a rich husband. The teaching gig for the twenty-six-year-old red head in Coronado, California was only a pit stop to something more rewarding, an escape from South Carolina family expectations.

When a far-flung resume hooked a job interview at Yellowstone National Park as assistant to the Head Geologist, Dr. George Ainslee, Christie grabbed it.

This was sad news to AC and Toad. Christie was the real deal: smart, passionate, and easy on the eyes. But they all realized fate had cast different lots for them all.

"So, let's party down!" volunteered Toad.

The big throw down was Jell-O shots all around to set the mood, then a set your hair on fire dancing and drinking binge till the sun came up. They left an imprint on that Coronado oyster bar that would be hard to beat.

It all started with the arrival of several bushels of live blue crabs.

Not just any crabs, but gnarly "Big Jimmies" measuring seven inches point to point across the shell; mean, nasty and covered in barnacles. They jostled, jumped, and snapped at anything within reach of their thirty-gallon wash tub prison.

To AC, this was too good to pass up.

"Hey Toad," AC prodded. "Tell 'em about the time you made a Yankee puke his lunch when you ate a live crab."

Toad was about half-way through his rendition of the feat; about how he held the crab's two pinchers apart and eye-to-eye with the crab, bit him in two, shell and all, when a patron slipped $10 bucks on the side by AC, challenged Toad to repeat the performance.

The crowd gathered around the washtub full of scrambling crabs. Goaded by alcohol and SEAL bravado, Toad reached for a crab with some steel tongs.

"No, no, not so fast," taunted his challenger. You got to grab him with your hands, and not that one. Grab that bad ass one over there, pointing to the largest male crab in the basket, its bluish black carapace crusted in barnacles, with seven-inch pinchers sporting hooked, red claws snapping with lethal intent.

Toad deftly snatched the big boy from behind, grasping the two rear swimmer legs. The incensed crab lashed and snapped his claws in futile defense.

When Toad quickly swapped his hold from the rear legs to the two formidable claws, his challenger again interrupted.

"Not this time. You got to bite him without holding the claws. You got to bite him straight on."

"Ain't no way," shouted a bystander.

"He's crazy" followed another.

The original $10 patron waved a wad of cash over his head, entreating the rowdy bar flies to step up. "Hundred bucks says he won't do it."

"I'll take that bet," challenged a beer bellied drunk. Another patron chimed in, "I want some of that action, too."

Toad looked over the crowd, left to right, saluting them with his last shot of mezcal, chewing the last drop of bravado from the tequila embalmed worm at the bottom of the bottle. He once again grabbed his adversary by its two back swimmers and looked the crab intensely into its two twitching stalked eyes. The crab bubbled and spit at Toad while the crowd chanted, "Do it, do it, do it!" Growing bets quickly changed hands.

Whiskey fevered, and never one to back off from a challenge, Toad held the angry crab mere inches from his face and with those lashing, snapping claws, he took a deep alcoholic breath and jammed the crab to his face.

Two things happened simultaneously. Toad bit two thirds through the crab's body, face on, and the crab latched onto Toad's face with both claws: one piercing Toad's right ear and the other his left chin and lip.

The crab squeezed, Toad cussed, and the crowd howled.

The crab's revenge was short lived. Toad shook his head violently from side to side like a big Labrador retriever with a death grip on a marsh 'coon, crab innards flying askew, but not its claws. In its death grip, the crab's claws remained rigidly attached to its tormentor.

Numbed to the pain, Toad shot-gunned a Budweiser to the howl and back slaps of the cheering crowd.

The juke box cranked up a Darius Rucker country tune as Toad pulled Christie onto the dance floor, juking and jiving, his still attached blue crab earrings all a-dangle, with blood leaking from the wounds.

All bets resolved; a solemn loser turned to AC.

"I wouldn't want that son of a bitch after my ass."

"Amen, brother."

Christie, out of breath, confronted AC. "Did you put him up to that?"

Toad mumbled out of the corner of his bleeding mouth while disengaging his crustaceous earrings, "AC, did you cover the spread?"

"Yep, fifteen to one," handing Toad his share of their winnings.

"HOO-YAH!"

Christie shoved them both away in dismay. "You guys are killing me! Y'all just ain't right."

When the three of them walked arm in arm out of the bar that next morning, it was a happy, sad mood. Toad squinted up at the morning sun with bloodshot eyes. "I didn't know there was that much liquor in all the world."

Christie chided, "Yeah, and you drank most all of it."

Mumbling and trying to wipe away the night's partying cobwebs, Toad lamented, "My head hurts."

AC couldn't resist the taunt. "Toad, you gotta have half a brain to have a headache."

Christie grabbed AC by the arm. "Hey guys, there's a selfie booth in the pavilion across the street. C'mon, we have to take a group shot."

"Christie, are you kidding me? I feel like shit."

"Just comb your hair and smile, boys." The three squeezed into the booth, Christie in the middle and the boys on either shoulder. Once the photos were in hand, she quipped, "There, Beauty and the Beasts. That didn't hurt, did it?"

Christie passed a copy to both guys, giving AC and Toad a loving peck on the cheek.

"No matter where fate finds the three of us, this picture will always keep us connected. Trouble seems to find you guys. AC, you keep Toad out of the brig. Toad, you watch AC's back. I know I can't always get a note to you in dog patch Iraq, or wherever the hell they send you, but you can always find me at Yellowstone. Love you guys."

After a last hug, Christie hailed her cab and drove away.

Two weeks later when the Team got its first real duty assignment, a nagging realization that had been haunting

AC's dreams outed itself. His granddaddy's Marine Corps blood ran deep in the family. It would not be denied. AC went to his commander and asked to be transferred to the Marine Corps. He wanted to fly fighter planes.

This floored Toad. First Christie left him, then his best friend betrayed him to become a jarhead Marine! The hurt hit him where bullets could not.

They had a heated argument, almost coming to blows. Only the interdiction of the rest of the SEAL crew kept them apart.

Toad's junkyard dog persona lashed out calling AC a bell ringing washout.

"You fuckin' jarhead."

Turning back to Toad as he got into a cab, AC uncharacteristically took a low cut at Toad.

"Squid" and drove away.

Eighteen months would pass as AC earned his Marine Corps pilot's wings and Toad kicked ass on other SEAL duty assignments...

CHAPTER 7: IN THE BLOOD

Twelve-year-old AC Collins spent his summers and Fall breaks from school on his grandfather's farm in a Colorado mountain valley doing what farm boys do: hiking the mountains and fishing for trout in the little stream meandering across the valley floor. Those lengthy breaks from a less idyllic home life were good medicine for the entire Collins family. AC's dad was a Vietnam vet with some tough combat history that wouldn't stay in the past. He suffered lingering PTSD issues that the young AC was not mature enough to cope with or to understand.

Long walks with his grandfather taught AC the ways of the wild. Wing shooting quail and pheasant with his grandfather taught young AC the reflexive skill of leading a moving target. These early lessons would prove to be invaluable in his later life. However, AC's fondest memories were the fireside camping trips where his grandfather told him enthralling tales of being a fighter pilot in WWII.

On one such trip the old man began, "The Japs were thick as fireflies on a summer night." Using his hands to simulate aerial combat, he explained dog fighting tactics and maneuvers. He would get lost in his memories as if he were back in the Pacific, 1942. His eyes glazed over with passion and vivid memories, and he would lapse into pilot-to-pilot conversations with his wingman, Jimmie Wright.

"Reaper One to Reaper Two, six zeros at our nine o'clock, 3,000 feet below. Let's take 'em from behind."

"Roger, Reaper One."

Then simulating his rolling bank and dive attack run, his breathing heavy with emotion, his hands clutching imaginary controls go to guns while describing his tracer bullets lacing two Zeros on his first pass.

"Reaper Two, zipped two Nips."

"Bingo Reaper One. I got two to starboard."

The two Wildcats' power dive overshot the two remaining Zeros.

The shoe was now on the other foot. The hunters had become the hunted. With the lighter, more maneuverable Zeros now on their six, the Wildcats had to go defensive. Earlier encounters in the war between the Japanese Zero and American aircraft often favored the Zero's tighter turning radius, enabling it to get inside the Wildcat's turn to acquire shooting advantage.

"Grandpa, how did you get away from the Zeros shooting at you."

The former Wildcat pilot, Lieutenant Ross Collins, explained. "We were getting our asses kicked by the Zeros early in the war. We could outrun and out gun them, but not in close combat. We just couldn't turn tight enough and fast enough to keep up with them. That all changed when Lieutenant Commander Thach devised a counter measure now called the Thach Weave. Two pilots crisscrossing each other's flight path could always cover the other's rear end, in a thatch weave pattern, giving the guy in the back of the weave a shot at anyone trying to close on the front plane. This two-pilot cover and shoot tactic offset any advantages the Zero had in close combat."

Lapsing back into memories forty years old, Lieutenant Ross Collins miked, "Gotta sky, Jimmie."

The two Wildcats went vertical, full power, maximum rate of climb, daring the Zeros to follow. Chasing sweet revenge, the Zeros took the bait. Breaking out above cloud cover, the Zeros tried to close within shooting range of the two Wildcats. At 32,000 feet the Zeros hit the ceiling of their performance envelope, while the Wildcats' 1,000 horse-power Supercharged Pratt and Whitney engines were still pulling strong to 35,000 feet. With engines coughing for air and sputtering into a powerless tail first fall, the Zeros had to roll out of their climb.

"Reaper One to Reaper Two. Gassed 'em, Jimmie. Follow their roll.

"Roger, Reaper One."

"We had 'em, and they knew it. Twisting and turning as they might, the two Zeros couldn't out-run our combined twelve .50 caliber machine guns tight on their ass.

"Splash two zeros." Lieutenant Collins pulled alongside his wing man, Jimmie Wright, cockpit to cockpit, giving a triumphant thumbs up.

"Both me and Jimmie earned our ACE that day."

Young AC, grasping every word, would often have to gently shake his grandfather's shoulder to snap him back to reality.

There was an unspoken vow between grandfather and grandson that they keep those fireside time travels a secret.

Some family members had voiced concerns about the old man's time out lapses.

After the war, Lieutenant Collins bought a de-commissioned Wildcat from a military surplus auction. Air racing old war birds was becoming popular with former combat pilots who had no more wars to fight, but still needed to feed the adrenaline rush of combat flying, the need for speed. Stripped bare of its guns and every possible ounce of disposable weight, his bird, sporting a snarling panther painted on both sides of its engine cowl, routinely took the field at these races. Later, marriage and family took center stage in Collin's life. The Wildcat was retired to the hay barn, defanged, wings folded back, hidden beneath dusty tarps, save for the occasional turning over of the engine to keep bearings and rubber seals oiled.

Years later the teenage grandson, AC, following one of his walks with his grandfather, was allowed to climb into the cockpit of the old plane. He played with the controls, throttle, and pedals, pretending he was the combat pilot of his grandfather's enthralling stories. The cockpit became a cocoon of solace for AC from teenage angst. There was a calming certainty about the smell and feel of old leather and engine oil.

It was on one of the fantasy trips to the barn that AC discovered several dusty wooden crates beneath and behind the Wildcat, tucked into a corner behind some farm tools. Unable to resist teenage curiosity, AC used a crowbar from a work bench to pop the lids on the crates. Wrapped in muslin cloth and coated in Cosmoline grease were six .50 caliber machine guns and a crate of ammunition. Entranced with the look and feel of the same guns his grandfather shot in the war, he was slow to realize the uncanny feeling of being watched. Slowly standing and turning from his magical find, AC found himself face to face with his grandfather. Feeling he had breached a sacred trust, AC stood, awaiting judgement. Instead of a harsh rebuke, the old man's stoic gaze slowly broke into a gentle smile, as if he and his grandson shared a secret no one else knew. Motioning AC to a hammer on the work bench, together they nailed the gun cases shut and returned them to their hiding place.

"AC, this is between us pilots, our bond. Just you and me. Understand?"

They walked out into the sunshine, never to mention the guns again. Years later, AC would inherit his grandfather's farm and its secrets.

One special Christmas Eve when AC's family spent the holidays with his grandparents, something happened that would be pivotal in AC's future. A knock on the front door opened to an older man about grandpa's age with snow on his shoulders matching his thinning white hair. The two men stood still for a quiet moment, then closed with a firm handshake and full embrace. Nothing was said for a few seconds, then turning to his family in the room behind him, with moist eyes and shaken voice, Grandpa Collins announced, "I want you all to meet my wingman, Jimmie Wright."

The two men had talked a couple of times over the years since the war, but their busy lives had never caught up with each other. Drinks were passed all around, and stories told over a delicious Christmas feast. No better a Christmas present could ever have walked through that farmhouse door, for no one could foresee that would be the last Christmas for First Lieutenant Wildcat pilot Collins.

"So, where you been all this time, Jimmie?"

"After the war I got into real estate on the west coast, lived a comfortable life until losing my wife Joan to cancer last year. Losing loved ones has become all too common at our age. I thought it was time to tighten up some loose ends, to see some old friends. Time to find my old flying buddy.

"My boy John just made Squadron Commander of VMFA-351 at Marine Corps Air Station, Beaufort, S.C. I spent a week with his family, enjoyed talking to the new guys on the flight line. Brought back a lot of old memories. I found a layover flight back to Los Angeles here in Boulder. I couldn't miss the chance to hook up one last time. You never know what's on your six."

"Jimmie, take a walk with me out to the barn. I want you to meet an old friend. AC, you, too."

Sadly, AC's dad, stuck in the 1960s, remained inside with the rest of the family.

Soon the entire valley shook to the thunderous roar of a 1,000 Wildcat horsepower.

Thirteen years later, and after his recent falling out with his SEAL buddy Toad Rawlings, the 25-year-old AC Collins was on his own mission. There is no Standard Operating Procedure for making the difficult inter-service transition from Navy SEALS to a career flying Marine Corps fighter planes. Even in the by the book military hierarchy it can come down to who you know, not what you know.

AC's completion of SEAL training was a huge advantage. No boot camp, no preliminaries, just surgically seeking the slender thread of a chance his application to flight school might find a favorable ear.

One of those three a.m. subconscious dreams, that often resolves questions and answers not realized in daylight, came to AC in a flash that jumped him straight out of his rack. Colonel John Wright, Pop Collin's wing man's son, squadron leader of VMFA-351, USMC; maybe, just maybe.

A quick Google search turned up a retired General John R. Wright, USMC, address Arlington, Virginia.

A twenty-hour drive and a knock on the door later, there was a response.

"General Wright, Sir?"

"Yes, and who wants to know?"

"Lt. AC Collins, Sir, grandson of Lt. Ross Collins, your father's wing man."

Raised eyebrows and a distant recollection proffered the firm handshake of a man still enjoying the rigors of his youth. "Little AC? Damn son, come on in. Whatcha drinking?"

The two men talked through several hours of drinks and a refrigerator lunch, finally getting to the crux of AC's visit.

"Sir, can you help me navigate the transition from the Navy SEALS to Marine Corps flight school?" AC explained his family's history, calling to him through his grandfather's stories.

General Wright paused to organize his thoughts. "Your Pops saved my Pop's ass several times. I wouldn't be here otherwise. I know a Lt. Colonel 'Bull' Hodges. Let me see what I can do. Son, you got to know I can open the door for you, but you got to walk through it on your own, pass the medical, rigorous testing, you know the drill. No special favors, even for a SEAL. Getting a front seat in the program means bumping someone else from their dream of becoming a naval aviator. There are only so many slots. You got to earn it, understood?"

"Absolutely, Sir. Understood. Thank you, Sir."

"Be careful what you ask for son. 'Road-y' for the ride?"

"Sir, bourbon and branch."

"And one more thing, AC. When you see Lt. Colonel Hodges, you have to stand to, and be ready to do what I'm about to tell you."

Minutes later AC turned from the doorway toward his car and muttered to himself; "Holy shit. I'm headed for the brig for sure."

Paperwork magically worked its way through the bureaucratic maze. Medical exams produced the coveted PQ (pilot qualification) to fly. All AC had to do was submit his AA form to make the leap from a back-seater designation to pilot. And he had to do it personally to Lt. Colonel "Bull" Hodges, a heavily decorated, legendary fighter pilot in the Corps.

Exhaling what was surely to be his last breath outside the brig, AC knocked on the door of Lt. Colonel Hodges' office. The cute little NCO with the push-up bra and skin-tight blouse routed him in. She wiggled her fine ass with a departing over the shoulder toss of her auburn hair and teasing blue eyes. None of it would pass a strict inspection.

AC came to attention in front of Hodge's desk.

Looking up from some papers on his desk and mouthing his words around a half chewed, twitching Havana, Lt. Colonel Hodges did a quick visual evaluation.

"At ease, Lt. Collins. What can I do for you?"

AC paused, choosing his words carefully. As instructed by General Wright, he straightened his spine and blurted out, "Sir, you are a homosexual."

The Havana grew still, one eye squinted as if placing AC into the reticle of his spotting scope. Hodges slowly raised up from his desk, leaning on arms stretched forward like a bulldog ready for a fight.

The cute NCO peered expectantly for a career beheading through the partly open doorway.

Instead of what AC surely believed to be a career ending death sentence, Hodges broke into a huge smile, pounded the desktop with a meaty fist and broke into a roaring belly laugh.

"Damn son. You maybe can't fly a fucking trashcan, but you sure got the balls for it. General Wright told me about you, a little character test, you might say. What you got there?"

Not sure of what to do, and holding his breath, AC stiffly handed his AA form to Lt. Colonel Hodges.

On quick review Hodges looked up at AC. "I'm going to sign off on this request for you. If you got the balls to come in here and call me a homosexual, you got the balls to fly my airplanes. Just don't fuck it up."

"Sir, yes, Sir. Understood, Sir."

"Dismissed."

One year later, having busted his ass surviving the intense training program called the pipeline, Lt. AC Collins made the final A-pool, the final cut, and earned his naval Aviator wings from the pilot training program in Pensacola,

Florida. During his training he was tagged with the call sign, Rooster from his off base extracurricular activities at a women's college campus, a popular hen house so to speak, with young naval aviators.

Two combat tours and two command grades later, Major AC Collins was assigned aboard the USS Nimitz in the Red Sea.

CHAPTER 8: GONE ROGUE

Pain is the best poultice for anger, like smacking one's thumb with a hammer supplants all other distractions. Ronnie Theodocius Toad Rawlings' hard edged loner personality did not react well to the break-up of the three-way friendship between himself, Christie Albright, and AC Collins. First Christie flew off to Yellowstone for a new job, then AC bailed out on him and the SEALS to fly Marine Corps fighter planes. The painful emotional risk of vesting himself in close personal relationships was a dark vestige holdover from his rough childhood fights with his drunken Marine Corps father.

Feeling betrayed by those closest to him, Toad launched a rage filled entry to the dark side where emotion became the enemy, where cold hard single-minded pursuit of only one objective became his religion. Toad applied to sniper school.

At age 27, Toad just made it inside the maximum age of 28 for entry into the sniper program. The burning psychological pain of betrayal crushed the temporary stress of sniper school physical training. Swimming 500 yards in 12 ½ minutes, 42 pushups in 2 minutes, 50 sit-ups in 2 minutes, 6 chin-ups on top of a mile and a half run, finishing with shooting 180 of 200 in Marksmanship using iron sights at 200 yards, found no purchase on Toad's ambitions. He, also, had to have near perfect Physical Fitness Test scores and completed the four-week Scout Recon school.

"Hell, let 'em knife fight a wild boar to see what real pain all is about."

The sniper program worked trainees twelve hours a day for three straight months, learning recon photography, satellite communications, how to move in and out of enemy territory undetected, and advanced marksmanship.

Called the old man by his team members, Toad was relentless in his pursuit of perfection. They drilled, they worked out, and they deprived themselves of the most basic human needs in an endless pursuit of one goal: Completing the mission! Staying alive was next on the list.

In their little time off from the twelve-hour daily grind, most trainees sought outside relief anywhere they could find it.

"Hey Toad, let's hit the town, you know, down some beers, score some chicks."

"Negative, got work to do."

Grinding himself to a razors edge on the wheel of perfection, Toad graduated from sniper school with the reputation as the toughest dog in the pound with top marks on the thousand-yard shooting range.

The following eighteen months found SEAL Team leader, Toad Rawlings, deployed to South and Central America on several missions to destabilize the drug cartels who were sending their deadly product to American cities. He and his spotter sometimes spent days alone in a hide overlooking a cocaine factory, or a boat yard fleet of narco-subs, or the compound of a cartel chief, waiting for the one shot that could bring down the operation, even if it was a temporary inconvenience. When one dirty dog goes down, another takes his place.

Tensions were running high in the drug underworld after the surgical terminations of several top cartel lieutenants. Word of a SEAL sniper team working the area brought down the heat on Toad's operation. The cartels hired a sniper of their own to rid them of the menace.

Toad and his spotter had methodically worked their way through the jungle to a rocky outcrop with an overview of a small valley crop of coca. On the opposite side of the valley was a brick and alabaster building of moderate size. Larger than any dwelling typical of the area; it was no ordinary home. With red terracotta roofing tiles and twin white portico columns, the place was surely the home of the local drug lord that DEA reported to be operating out of the area. Good intel, correct mapping coordinates, and a single lane dirt road entering the valley from both ends allowed no other motorized access. It was a perfect funnel point for isolating the SEALS intended prey.

Toad's spotter ranged possible targets.

"Front porch, 800 meters. Corner fence post, 575. Boulder at six o'clock, 125." Toad took it all down on his range card.

Day turned to night. Nothing. Dark crawly things, jungle noise and finally dogs barking. Roosters began calling in the new day. Carefully, moving as slow as the surrounding greenery, they capped the canteen following a couple of MREs, rolled over to piss, and back on the scope.

Shortly after sunrise, an enclosed jeep emerged from the far side of the jungle and pulled to a stop at the front of the hacienda.

Toad snuggled into his prone shooting position and whispered to his spotter over his right shoulder.

"Got him, 780 meters. Audio up."

Spotter, Chief Joe Duncan, flicked the "on" switch to the small directional listening dish brought just for that purpose.

Toad made his adjustments. Range, 780 meters, slight left-to-right breeze. One in twelve twist, minimal bullet drift. In the shooter's zone, he slowed his breathing, finger on the trigger of his silenced 7.62 MK-11 sniper rifle, awaiting his chance.

Four men got out of the Jeep, three were hired Sicarios with automatic weapons. The gunmen turned outward from the jeep in protective positions. The fourth man, in dark clothes, white straw hat, and carrying a suitcase, approached the hacienda.

Into the field of view of his Night Force scope stepped a man from inside the house. Dressed in a full white suit and a bright red tie, the man was accompanied by two gunmen. He walked down the steps and approached the straw hat.

The two-man exchange was brief and conclusive.

Toad whispered into his headset, "Joe, you gettin' all that?"

"Roger that; he's our man."

The suitcase changed hands with a subservient bow to the white suit and red tie. With a nod from red tie toward the door behind him, six men emerged from the hacienda with three large boxes, which they loaded into the back of the jeep.

To seal the deal, straw hat man reached out to shake the hand of the red tie man who suddenly and violently lurched backwards toward the steps in a crumpled heap, with blood spurting from his bright red tie. All guns began wildly firing in every direction. In rapid succession, one, two, then three gunmen assumed a like position beside their dead chief. Chaos reigned.

"Time to move, Joe." But just as Toad readied to tap out his spotter, he heard the snap of a round striking above his right ear. Then he saw the glint of a weapon above and behind the hacienda.

"Sniper twelve o'clock. Joe. Joe?"

Returning three quick bolt action rounds to the glassy reflection produced a body rolling out of his hide to the rocks below.

"Got that nose picker."

Turning to his spotter, Toad found Joe stone dead from a head wound.

In a tortured dead man's carry, Toad made the two-hour hump to his extraction point and back to the world.

CHAPTER 9: THE SWORD OF ALLAH

Fatwa from Nazer bin Hamd:

"Weapons of mass destruction will kill the infidels on whom they fall, regardless of whether they are fighters, women, or children. They will destroy and burn the land. The arguments of permissibility are many."

A crowd of Al Qaeda fighters and supporters gathered in the courtyard of a Pakistani mosque where Abou Aziz, Afghan leader of a powerful Al Qaeda faction, addressed his followers.

"Brothers of jihad, soldiers under Allah, we welcome Brother Kamal Rashid back to his homeland. He has been away many months in the land of the Great Satan. He comes to us with great news.

"Brothers, we have been at war with the infidels and pagans for many years now. From the days of our forefathers who fought them in the Crusades, through the division of our lands under their imperial transgressions, taking our homelands, redrawing our boundaries separating brother from brother, fighting the Russians, and now the Americans in every way in every place. We honor Allah, blessed be his kingdom, as we fight them now.

"We pierced the pride of the Americans when we bombed the Aegis Cruiser Cole. We killed many of their soldiers in bombing their barracks in Beirut. We fought them in the mountains of Afghanistan. Under the leadership of the great Osama bin Laden, Allah rest his soul, we smote them in New York City on 9-11. We kill the Americans in war, we kill them with roadside bombs, we bleed their strength and treasure with our martyrs in their midst. But, dear Brothers, despite all our strength and the righteous hand of Allah, we have not defeated them. We cannot defeat them face to face in battle. They are too strong, and they are too many. They kill from afar with their drones and their secret raids, dropping silent as death from the night to kill and capture our leaders. Their soldiers march across our dead bodies as a man walks across short grass.

"Brothers, the Great Satan is too great an enemy to bring down with these pinpricks. Some have said we can eat away at them as termites eat away the foundations of great buildings; by assimilating our Muslim brothers into their societies to eat at the fabric of their pagan lifestyles. Our mosques can be training and recruitment grounds to build an army within, an army of termites for jihad, by the will of Allah.

"While Allah's patience is endless, the Americans are even more quickly seeking us out with their war machines. They kill our newly elected leadership faster than we can replace them. I have just these last few months taken the place of my cousin Hamid Aziz, who was taken from us by a drone as he knelt in prayer. My very life is now measured in months, for as soon as they learn of me, a drone will come for me, as well.

"No, my brothers. We need a new savior, a new plan such as the Americans have never seen. A plan so great, so powerful, and by The Sword of Allah, so terrible as to smite the Great Satan and bring him to his knees before Allah, in one mighty blow.

"Dear Brothers, our Brother from America, Brother Kamal Rashid, has come to us with such a mighty weapon. Please listen now to your Brother."

Rashid paused carefully. "Brothers in Allah. A weapon, more powerful than all others, lies within our grasp to attack the heart of the Great Satan. Its name is Yellowstone. Beneath Yellowstone National Park, in America's heartland, lies the beating heart of the Beast. A volcano, the largest in all the world, so powerful that it alone could deliver a devastating blow so great that it would cripple America forever and drive the infidels from our lands for all time. We have but to awaken the Beast within Yellowstone and Allah will blanket two thirds of America under feet of ash and devastation. We will kill the infidels by the millions, lay waste to their lands, and create a power vacuum not seen in five hundred years. The time of Arab rule, of Sharia Law has come. The Great Satan will be no more!"

Cheers of "Allahu Akbar" and sporadic gunfire into the air celebrated this new turning of history's page.

"Brother Kamal, how may we accomplish this great feat?" asked Aziz.

"With Allah's help, I will martyr myself to place a small nuclear bomb against the underbelly of Yellowstone."

"But where will we get such a bomb?" another asked.

"I have heard of it myself, from Osama bin Laden, that after the Americans brought down the Russian Empire, he paid Chechen rebels and KGB traitors thirty million dollars in cash, and another six million dollars of heroin to purchase twenty suitcase size nuclear bombs. They are small enough to be carried by one man, and powerful enough to destroy an entire New York City block. A two-kiloton nuclear explosion, placed at just the right geologic pressure point, will be enough to waken the volcano under Yellowstone. Osama has hidden these devices deep inside a cave in the northern Tora Bora mountains. He called them The Swords of Allah and has hidden them until the time is right. Brothers, that time is now!

"Come, my Brothers in jihad. Now is the time to make Al Qaeda relevant on the world stage again. Let us convene in council to discuss how this thing may be done. By the will of Allah, let us show the infidels the meaning of terror!"

Shouts of "Allahu Akbar! Allahu Akbar! Allahu Akbar!" rocked the courtyard outside the mosque.

CHAPTER 10: KIDNAPPED

If patience is a virtue, it must surely have been invented by an Arab. Where the West measures time by the calendar, by Saturday's tee time, or the opening of the stock market, the Arab mind can wait patiently for a thousand years. All is under Allah's infinite control.

Tuesday started off the same as every other day of the week. Park staff routines, as meticulous and predictable as their lab work at Yellowstone National Park, began early.

Dr. Ainslee's kitchen lights, at his refurbished farmhouse outside of town, came on at 6:30 a.m. sharp every morning. At 6:45 he walked to the mailbox for the morning paper. His car left the driveway at 8:00 for the thirty-minute drive to his office in Jackson, Wyoming, where a security gate isolated the offices and labs from the public. A working lunch was taken every Wednesday at the Cowboy Bar & Grill on Main Street from 12:00 to 1:00

111

with the Park's Assistant Geologist, Dr. Christie Albright. Other days Dr. Ainslee ate a homemade sandwich at his desk. Their day ended officially at 6:00 p.m.

George Ainslee had not always been the pencil necked geek in the white lab coat seen at the Yellowstone Visitor Center and orientation film. Fifty years earlier Private First-Class George W. Ainslee had been a jungle humping grunt with the United States Marine Corps fighting in the jungles of Vietnam. He was a Tunnel Rat. His wiry, five-foot-five-inch frame snaked through many a dark Vietcong tunnel maze with a flashlight in one hand and a Colt .45, 1911 A-1 pistol in the other. Regarded by the Vietcong as the best of America's armed forces, tunnel rats were careful not to do anything that would dull their finely tuned senses of touch, smell, hearing; nothing to alert the enemy of their presence. No drugs, no cologne, aftershave, or even chewing gum. When called upon by combat engineers to explore a suspicious hole in the ground, the tunnel rat's strongest asset was the ability to focus absolutely, denying sweat and panic laden claustrophobia, intent upon feeling their way through total darkness, booby traps, and ambush from enemy soldiers hiding in the dark. Very few of these one hundred specialized soldiers, designated as tunnel rats, survived the war. Most of them died scared and alone, deep underground, impaled, shot, bombed, or buried alive. They volunteered for the assignment in return for an extra fifty dollars a month hazardous duty pay, and the admiration of their fellow soldiers who wouldn't do the job for a truckload of money.

Specialist George Ainslee earned medals for heroism as a tunnel rat at the beginning of the Tet Offensive of 1968. Tet was the Vietnamese New Year surprise attack by the North Vietnamese on the South. The massive underground tunnel system housed thousands of enemy troops, built to resist French occupation of Vietnam, was later to become the nerve center of the Viet Cong military.

Tunnel rat Ainslee was part of a tunnel search and destroy operation. He and his tunnel rat German Shepard cleared a tunnel leading to and supporting senior Viet Cong military staff. Ainslee and his dog killed a dozen enemy soldiers and retrieved a treasure trove of documents, exposing enemy strength and troop movements. This action resulted in a major VC unit, in his USMC area of operations in I Corps, surrendering before the first day of the TET fight.

After the war he never found a wife to share his nightmares, to hold him tight in the wee hours when the smothering memories came flooding back. For all the years since the Vietnam War, George Ainslee had been married to his ghosts.

On his office wall hung a picture of eighteen-year-old George with several of his wartime buddies. George was the only one of them to make it home. On his desk was a ball cap, the visor reading, Born to Dig. As a geologist at Yellowstone, George could face down his demons by exploring interesting holes in the ground with pick and trowel instead of flashlight and pistol in the distant rat tunnels of Vietnam. His favorite song, often heard wafting from his office, was "Paint it Black," by the Rolling Stones.

"I see a red door and I want it painted black.
No colors anymore, I want them to turn black.
I see the girls walk by dressed in summer clothes,
I have to turn my head until my darkness goes. "

The fated tune became a euphemism for soldiers' desperate search for some place to hide their souls from the Hell that was the 'Nam.

"I look inside myself and see my heart is black.
I see my red door and must have it painted black.
Maybe then I'll fade away and not have to face the facts.
It's not easy facin' up when your world is black. "

Sixty-eight-year-old George Ainslee, still slim and trim, lightly balding, with a neatly trimmed beard, was a visible mainstay of the Park staff. His simple smile and charming manner put everyone at ease. He'd been to Hell and painted it black.

Dr. Christie Albright shared rent with another park employee in a small duplex several blocks outside Jackson's tourist district. Even there, rent was not cheap, especially on a government salary. Her life was all about her work. She dated occasionally, but most of the new faces coming through Jackson were adrenalin junkies out to prove their immortality on mountain tops or raging rivers. They reminded her too much of her old friends, AC and Toad.

Together with Dr. Ainslee, Christie's job at Yellowstone was to monitor and study the Park's natural assets, most notably the prehistoric volcano beneath it. To them, the park's volcanic heartbeat made it almost a living, breathing thing. Seismic monitors recorded every tremor and rumble. Temperatures for the park's numerous hot pools were charted over time to measure continuity and warn of any pending geologic activity. The park's underground anatomy was mapped with small black powder charges that bounced sound waves off varying underground strata and onto their scrolling computer charts.

The inveterate digger, Dr. Ainslee took every opportunity to also chart the park's underground cavern and magma vent systems. The former tunnel rat had a passion for caving in his spare time.

Patient Arab eyes watched all this for many weeks, recording Dr. Ainslee's routine in detail.

That September day was different. At the usual 6:00 p.m., Dr. Ainslee's car exited the security gate, but he was not alone. There were four people in the car: Dr. Ainslee, Dr. Albright, and two junior assistants. Dr. Ainslee would surprise the two assistants whose promotions would be announced at work the next day. George and Christie planned a small, intimate dinner party to celebrate the big occasion, held at a cozy inn several miles out of town. Dr. Ainslee concocted the ruse that he needed their help to move some monitoring equipment to the next day's job site.

Seemingly routine small office talk turned to the weather report on the radio. It was starting to snow.

"Looks like another big blow coming through," Christie observed. "All that Cascade moisture rolling in from the mountains to the west meeting that arctic blast pouring down from Canada is gonna dump a shit load of snow on Yellowstone."

"This light dusting is gonna get really nasty, really fast." George replied, slowing the car slightly.

A light crunching sound of freshly fallen snow under the tires followed the car out of the compound gate and onto the highway.

This departure from the Arab plan had not been anticipated. It was too late to change what had been set in motion weeks ago. Abdoul Mustafa had his orders. As Dr. Ainslee's headlights swept around a bend in the road, he saw a truck pulling a hay wagon jackknifed across the highway.

One of the grad students pointed out the front window. "Damn, look at that."

When Dr. Ainslee pulled to a stop to lend assistance, two men rushed the car from opposite sides, shouting in Arabic and motioning for everyone to get out of the car. Both carried machine pistols. It was apparent Mustafa's two younger assailants were unsure of what to do next about the unexpected passengers.

The brandishing of automatic weapons awakened fifty years of buried fury in George Ainslee. Out of the darkness where he had sought to bury them came flashbacks of black pajama clad soldiers herding innocent villagers to slaughter; of draping bloody rain ponchos over the dead faces of buddies he'd shared breakfast with hours earlier. Former Private First-Class Ainslee made a grab for the Smith and Wesson .357 magnum bear gun in his driver side door pocket. In the instant his hand found its re-assuring grip, a ripping pistol butt to the base of his neck rendered him mute.

The older Mustafa briskly shoved a stunned Dr. Ainslee and Dr. Albright face first up against the hay wagon, and using nylon zip ties, bound their hands behind their backs.

In perfect English Mustafa warned them. "Do as you are told, if you want to live."

Then, without warning, he turned, and machine gunned the two young lab assistants. The muffled thump, thump, thump of a silenced muzzle whisked away on the wind, left two dead bodies in a snow drift beside the road.

Thinking she, too, was about to die Christie lashed out in the only way she could, suddenly turning and shouting, "YOU FUCKING COWARD", driving her right knee into Mustafa's crotch. Rising painfully and with a great desire to kill her right then and there, he backhanded her, knocking her to the ground and bloodying her lip. He shouted to one of the other assailants in Arabic, who produced a bottle of liquid and a cloth, soaking the rags and smothering the two captives' faces with it. In seconds they lay unconscious on the ground.

Dr. Ainslee had been the sole target of the operation. Christie Albright and the two unfortunate assistants just happened to be in the wrong place at the wrong time. She would provide negotiating leverage as a hostage. The two lab assistants were simply in the way.

Both captives were lifted and shoved into a specially prepared hollow inside one of the huge round hay bales. Mustafa headed the truck and trailer north. The other men followed behind at a discreet distance, later to ditch Dr. Ainslee's car in a roadside ravine. The two geology assistants were left mysteriously and unaccountably dead by the side of the road.

Hours later and safely across the border into Saskatchewan, the innocuous load of cattle hay pulled to a midnight stop at an abandoned farmstead turned operations center; the night's snow fall having fully erased all trace of their arrival.

Welcoming new arrivals on the snowfall, Abdul Mustafa was addressed by his master who commissioned him with a quote from the Koran, "Go with Allah. Those who inhabit paradise will wear fine silk garments of green." Having executed his part in a larger plan, Mustafa prepared to meet a colleague for a long ride back to Toronto and underground anonymity.

Kamal Rashid and six true believers prepared for their siege on the Great Satan.

The next day Jackson was abuzz with the news of the disappearance of Drs. Ainslee and Albright and the two grisly murders on the highway. Already a case to be handed over to the FBI, recent chatter intercepted by the NSA about a possible terrorist act, and something called the Sword of Allah caused an uneasy churning in Dan Shields' belly.

While national security trumped all other considerations, the apparent kidnapping of his two new friends put a different twist to the already bizarre affair. Dan Shields would personally lead the investigation.

The FBI searched the homes of both Dr. Ainslee and Dr. Albright, interviewed friends, neighbors, and Christie's roommate. Nothing. No known enemies, no financial or personal problems, nothing unusual in any way. Dan was drawn to a photo of Christie and two men in military fatigues. Her smile was infectious, wholesome; a strange thought to have in a moment like this. Dan's job had never allowed time for a wife, or really any other life outside the

Bureau. He shook his head as if to clear an unfamiliar cobweb. Emotional involvement was not an agency approved investigative procedure.

"Damn, son, get your head back in the game," he scolded himself.

Something about this case just didn't fit. Two abstract acts with no apparent connection.

Turning this over and over in his mind, Shields' jaws suddenly clenched with intuitive insight. That queasy gut feeling was whispering to him again. It whispered the name Kamal!

CHAPTER 11: THE COLOMBIAN CONNECTION

Half a world away from Yellowstone, a wild and muddy river winds its way to the sea, beneath verdant limestone cliffs, through tangled mangrove swamps, from deep within the heart of a wild South American jungle. Known only to drug smugglers and corrupt government officials is a secret facility with its own power plant and construction docks. Tethered nearby, the last of the ocean blue and green camouflage paint was being applied to a small, clandestine submarine known in the drug trade as a Narco-submarine.

Accepting no small chance of being killed on sight, an unheralded newcomer, by way of bribery and payoffs to other dark members of the world-wide terror network, risked death to make a desperate connection pivotal to his master plan.

Beneath a half-acre of camouflaged netting strung high in the forest canopy was a make-shift command center. Heavily armed men in tree stands overlooked the entire operation, 24/7. Guard dogs continually monitored the perimeter. Under a thatched cabana, cooled by two slow, squeaking ceiling fans, sat an unassuming man busy with his paperwork, doodling on a notepad and chewing a half-smoked stogie.

An aid approached his boss carefully, pointing to the construction dock.

"Kamal Rashid from Pakistan wishes to speak with Señor Sangre about an important matter.

Señor Sangre shifted his dark green sunglasses and coolly lifted his eyes from beneath a weathered straw hat. Extending his arm toward a chair, he bid Kamal to sit. Turning to his aid, he commanded in Spanish, "Bring coffee and sweet cake."

Well versed on the histories of each other, the meeting was arranged through others known to them both. The two men, each from different sides of the world, from different cultures and languages, shared a bond in addition to the English language: the brotherhood of international mayhem.

After the requisite introductions and courteous small talk, Señor Sangre and Kamal Rashid got down to business.

"And what does my Arab brother from desert lands need of a submarine?" Señor Sangre asked.

"We have a common interest, brother. You seek great profits poisoning The Great Satan with your heroin and cocaine. I seek justice for a thousand years of infidel atrocities thrust upon my people and our lands. America, the Great Satan, is our common enemy."

Cutting right to the bottom line, Señor Sangre asked, "And how may I profit from helping you get your revenge?"

"You need raw heroin to make your product. I can offer you a nearly unlimited source of the purest heroin from the poppy fields of Afghanistan and Pakistan."

Señor Sangre leaned back in his chair and exhaled a blue ring of smoke from a fine Cuban cigar, his body language suggesting to Rashid that he had reached a favorable ear.

"And in return?"

"I need the submarine about to be completed, and a competent crew."

"And just what do you intend to do with my submarine?"

"Jihad's freedom fighters rely on the help of all the world's oppressed to battle the Great Satan. The submarine is but a small part of a larger plan, which I cannot disclose to you at this time. Rest assured in this, my brother, America will know the sting of Allah's revenge."

"Tell me, Señor Sangre, I am curious; why, in this God forsaken jungle, have you the need for the many guns surrounding this place."

"There is no place on this planet in which we can safely hide from the men with green faces. No one can know when a silent bullet will reach out for us from beyond the best eyes. They come for us like the jaguar, day, or night. Although I am a man of great wealth and pride, I dare not stand out from my laborers as a target, as you can see." For emphasis, Señor Sangre waved his arm toward the simply dressed all about the compound.

"Men with Green faces? Who are these mystical men you fear so greatly? They are just men like you and I, are they not?"

"No, my friend. They are the Devil's own angels; they are of the Great Satan. They are U. S. Navy SEALS. When I was a younger man full of bravado and revolutionary dreams in Panama, I saw first-hand how they decapitated our leadership, routed General Noriega, and snuffed out the light of revolution. A group of these men in small teams of six carried more firepower in their Stoner and M-60 machine guns than an entire regiment of my best fighters. No. No more for me. Thereafter, I fled to these jungles to pursue my own ambitions, in anonymity."

Señor Sangre composed himself. "Yes, it is good that America fears us both, for in fear lies strength. I will help you get your revenge. And after today, you will never see or hear from me again. A third party will handle the shipments. I will remain invisible, understood?"

Señor Sangre leaned forward in his chair. "Come, let us make plans."

Kamal closed the deal. "My people will arrange for the first shipment of product to be delivered to the destination of your choice by the first of the month and..."

At the NSA headquarters in Langley, Virginia a Code Red scrambled together the top brass from NSA, CIA, and the FBI.

An abstract report was called in to the FBI from a motel operator in Jackson Hole, Wyoming. A vacationing family found a cryptic message hidden in the Gideon's Bible in their motel room and gets immediate attention. The hidden message, neatly cross folded four times, was placed at Revelations 16:13 in a similar manner to the Jeremiah 29:11 verse code used in an earlier clandestine communication leading to the 2001 attack on the World Trade Center.

Jeremiah 29:11 reads, "For I know the plans I have for you, plans to prosper you, not to harm you, plans to give you hope and a future."

The Revelations verse 16:13; "And I saw three unclean spirits like frogs come out of the Mouth of the Dragon, and out of the Mouth of the Beast, and out of the mouth of false prophets."

Consulting religious scholars familiar with both bible verses shed no light on their abstract meanings, other than to agree with what the FBI already knew. They were sign posts in a foreboding journey with meanings known only to those intended to find them.

This new message suggested that the same network code was being used to coordinate another pending terrorist attack. Under the scrutiny of ultraviolet light examination, the FBI found a hidden phone number on the back of the note. Forensically bare of any other tangible information such as fingerprints, or traces of saliva, sweat, or any other usable solvents, it was all the FBI had to work with.

An international cell phone intercept of the same number, originating in Islamabad, Pakistan and tracked to a suspected radical Muslim mosque in Toronto, Canada, resulted in the arrest of one Abdoul Mustafa. Brought before his captors in orange jump suit and handcuffs, Mustafa was interrogated behind the one-way glass window of a holding cell. The open mike brought the FBI interpreter's questions and Mustafa's answers to the group.

"You can speak your tongue. I know your pagan English."

The FBI biometric recorder, Cross Match, had already taken Mustafa's fingerprints, eye scan, and facial recognition scan identifying him as one of several bad actors loosely connected to several recent terrorist events.

His name was familiar to the NSA. This time was different, though. The intercepted cell phone call connected Mustafa to something called The Sword of Allah.

Dan Shields did not like the sound of that. Too many moving parts to something he could only feel but not yet understand.

Preferring again to risk pink slip over toe tag, Shields signed off on the order to put Mustafa through deep interrogation.

"No piss-ant, politically correct bullshit this time. There's something happening here, and I aim to find out what it is!"

Mustafa finally broke after two weeks of intense interrogation; sleep deprivation, time warping strobe lights, and a relentless, pounding monotone noise that numbed his mind and soul to the very core. He looked disheveled and dejected, his eyes vacant of emotion. He was an empty shell to be picked clean by the FBI's best miners of information. He admitted there was a terrorist plan to smuggle a suicide team into San Francisco Bay aboard a small narco-sub. Even after repeated water boarding, Mustafa stuck to his story.

"He doesn't know the specific details, only that it's supposed to happen in the month of September on the anniversary of 9/11."

Summoning the last of a zealot's ebbing strength, Mustafa shouted, "This will be our greatest victory over the infidels. You cannot stop us any more than you can stop the drugs coming into your country. Allah will have his revenge. Allahu Akbar!"

With only two weeks until the eleventh of September, Homeland Security and the FBI put on a full court press of all available resources to locate and stop any suspicious ocean traffic off the west coast.

Dan Shields consulted with his Homeland Security counterpart, "What more do we know about these narco-subs?"

"They're damn hard to catch. Most are small by submarine standards, about eighteen meters long. They have an extremely low waterline, and because they're made mostly of fiberglass, are almost invisible to sonar and radar. They can be operated by a crew of only two or three, are fully submersible, and can carry a payload of around ten tons. That much cocaine has a street value of one hundred million dollars, so the two-million-dollar cost to build one is chump change to these guys. Most of the subs are scuttled after they offload the drugs onto speed boats several miles from the coast. Catching one is more luck than skill."

"Do they have the range to get from Columbia, South America, all the way up our coast to San Francisco?" Shields asked. "Is Mustafa's plan doable?"

"I'm afraid so. The few we have intercepted ran on diesel motors and had a fuel/cruising range estimated to be about thirty-two hundred nautical miles."

"Shit! Columbian drug lords, Mexican smugglers, and international terrorists all working together. What a perfect nexus of crime."

"Ten-ton payload, you say. That could be dozens of suicide fighters or ten tons of high explosives like C-4, cordite, or simply the poor man's choice of fertilizer mixed with kerosene. Can you imagine how much damage ten tons of cordite could do? What about the Bay Bridge or commercial shipping?"

"Taking out a luxury cruise liner with a couple of thousand tourists makes a fat target, too."

Shields thought for a few seconds. "Scramble your guys and start hardening potential targets in the San Francisco Bay Area. We have to throw a wide net if we're going to stop these guys."

U.S. Navy boat and air patrols, as well as Coast Guard cutters, made continuous sorties up and down the thousand-mile coast from Baja to the Oregon border. A dozen hapless smugglers and lowlifes were caught in the dragnet, but not the prize for which they were hoping.

Inwardly the black heart of Abdoul Mustafa smiled a wicked smile. The trap had been laid, and time was getting short.

Hunkered deep down at the bottom of San Francisco Bay in silent anticipation sat a thirty-foot-long tube of jihadist retribution. The original Columbian crew had been executed and summarily dumped overboard two days cruise out from its jungle berthing. It was time enough for its new crew to master operational capability, their last admonition from Kamal Rashid still ringing in their ears. "Go with Allah." They patiently awaited their date with martyrdom.

CHAPTER 12: FURLOUGH

The summer heat was yielding to colorful Fall in the Teton Mountains of Wyoming and Major AC Collins was enjoying a hard-earned two-week leave. His nerves were frayed from a month aboard an aircraft carrier teaching a group of young pilots the delicate art of touch-and-go landings. Navigating wind speed, ship speed, wind shear, and the invisible bow wave of compressed air in front of the Nimitz are critical flying skills pilots must learn to survive in the extremely dangerous environment of the pitching deck of the carrier. IIe was in dire nccd of feeling firm ground beneath his feet again, to get back to his mountains. He hooked up with a bunch of adrenalin junkies in a climbing club calling themselves The Yellowstone Peak Baggers. Each member kept a detailed log of every climb and peak conquered as a testament to courage, earning bragging rights, like a big game hunter with his trophy wall.

The two-week climbing trip began with El Capitan in Yosemite National Park, then on to Cloud Peak in Wyoming, easily visible from Yellowstone. What made these two peaks so compelling to dedicated climbers is that they are two of only a handful in North America that exceed thirteen thousand feet in elevation. It takes special equipment and advanced climbing skills to bag these two. Not surprisingly, the mental tools required to excel in the sport are like those of fighter pilots. They must be able to manage fear and perform at extremely high levels in stressful situations where lesser men fail.

The El Capitan climb, while meticulous and dangerous, went without a hitch. Not so with Cloud Peak.

The Cloud Peak ascent began at 2:00 a.m. The first four hours of the twenty-hour climb would be in the dark, but on a relatively mild trail. The game plan was to make five thousand feet by sunrise. Topping out at thirteen thousand feet mid-day, taking the requisite baggers' trophy group picture as proof of summiting, and the climb back to safety would consume the final sixteen hours, or so they planned.

They did not plan on a failed pylon and a broken leg.

Twelve climbers began the trek, nine men, and three women. Matt Grimes was the Climb Guide assigned by the Park Service to shepherd The Peak Baggers excursion. He was by far the most experienced climber in the bunch, having already done Everest and Kilimanjaro. The others were experienced weekenders. Major AC Collins bounced in for the occasional climb whenever he got the chance.

The predawn preliminaries went well, sorting gear, adjusting to the gradual elevation change, and settling their climbing legs. Small talk gave way to increased focus on footing and breathing as they tackled the tougher parts of the trail.

At the five-thousand-foot marker, Matt Grimes settled onto a convenient boulder.

"Listen up, everyone. Let's grab a fifteen-minute break. Take some water and chow. Check each other's rigging. From here to the summit and back we will tie off in ten foot-increments. The trail is well marked with elevation posts and preset pylons to navigate the tougher sections. Everyone works from one pylon to the next, unclipping to move forward, and re-clipping to the next as a safety check for the climber below."

From the ten-thousand-foot marker to the summit at thirteen thousand feet, the mountain was covered in snow, the most treacherous part of the climb. The leapfrog of tethered climbers finally reached the summit at 2:00 p.m. They shared a celebratory bottle of wine and took photos, but there was no time to linger. The relatively mild temperature of fifteen degrees at the summit would drop to twenty below zero after sunset.

The euphoria of triumph often leads to a lessening of caution, even for experienced climbers. The snowbanks and ice crevasses of Everest routinely attest to this fact with an annual body count of dozens of careless or unprepared climbers.

The descent from Cloud Peak began as had many others.

Matt Grimes nodded his head to the Northern skyline, commenting to AC, "I don't like the looks of that storm front moving in from the north. It'll be on us in a couple of hours. We got to get a hustle on. Let the less experienced climbers go first. You be the lead anchor. I'll bring up the rear belaying those in front as the group leap frogs down the trail they broke on the ascent."

"Roger that," agreed AC, turning to address the group.

"Everyone, listen up. You all follow the footsteps of the man in front of you. I'm on lead with Matt running drag from behind."

Just five hundred feet below the summit a huge chunk of snow and ice, disturbed by passing climbers, broke free with a cracking groan, hurtling downward onto the climbers below.

AC heard it first, turning to yell a warning to Matt Grimes; he was too late. The impact slammed into Matt, knocking him loose from his rope anchors. Mute with horror, his body careened into the next climber down line, jerking him from his anchor, too. The two falling climbers threatened to drag the entire group off the mountainside to certain death. Only the painful crunch of breaking bone halted the unraveling fall when Grimes crashed into a rocky crevasse, effectively using his body as a wedge to re-lock the group to the mountainside.

Shock gave way to action as AC took command of the situation.

"Is everyone OK? Matt? Matt! Everybody, count-off."

"Matt's hurt, AC. He's unconscious and his right leg is badly broken. We got to get him off this mountain."

No second look was needed to realize the severity of the injury; jagged bone punched through Matt's outer legging; his right leg twisted at a bizarre angle to his body. Fortunately, there was only minor bleeding. The femoral artery had not been punctured.

AC took Matt's backpack and dug out his radio.

"Emergency call to Mountain Rescue. Matt Grimes is down, broken leg, five hundred feet below the summit."

"Rescue One to AC. You got eighty knots of storm headed your way. Too rough for air rescue. No level landing zone, either. You have to get him below ten thousand feet."

AC paused to formulate a plan. "Roger, Rescue One."

AC instructed the others using ropes to rig a make-shift body sling to rappel Matt down the mountain. An hour later he realized; with Matt in tow, the group would not make ten thousand feet before dark and the approaching storm.

"Rescue One. I'm sending the rest of the group down. I will bivouac overnight with Grimes. I'm digging a snow cave at eleven thousand feet on the south face."

"Roger, bivouac. We'll collect your party at that flat outcropping at eight thousand feet. Update your status hourly. Remember, there's a severe risk of hypothermia and hypoxia."

"Roger. I took on extra oxygen from two descending climbers. The group can share air to get to the eight thousand pick up. AC, clear."

AC used his climbing ax to dig out a cave large enough to hold the two men. It backed up to a large rock face, sheltering them from the frigid wind and fast dropping temperatures. Lined with both men's emergency space blankets the cave was a relatively well insulated shelter. Body heat and a small single burner alpine Sterno stove quickly brought the inside temperature up to a balmy thirty degrees.

"Rescue One, we're buttoned up for the night. Grimes is conscious but hurting. Will advise. AC, out."

Matt Grimes grimaced through clinched teeth, "Well AC, I guess I really mucked it up, didn't I?"

"Could have been a lot worse."

"Still can. We aren't outa this mess yet."

"You just keep thinking about that cute little divorcee who's been giving you the big-eye all week long. She'll be down the mountain waiting for you. Hang on, buddy. Here, swallow this handful of pain killers and eat some caffeinated chocolate. Got to keep you awake 'till daylight.

AC set an AM alarm on his wristwatch.

In the flickering light of the pocket stove, AC pulled out the picture of himself, Toad, and Christie. Somehow the warmth of good memories staved off the numbing cold and offered a restful place for his thoughts as he tried to get a few fitful hours of sleep, always keeping an ear tuned to Grimes' steady breathing. Daylight and the wake-up buzz of his wrist alarm stirred him from a soft slumber. He gave Matt a wake-up nudge and slipped the photo back into his jacket pocket. "Hey buddy, it's go-time. The radio chirped to life as AC prepared to put his half-frozen feet back onto the trail.

"Rescue One to AC. How's it hangin', AC?"

"We're still here, Rescue One. What's for breakfast?"

"We're dropping a four-man team at the rally point at ninety-five hundred feet. They'll meet you on the trail."

"Roger, Rescue One."

Imminent rescue gave Matt Grimes the strength to hang on and AC to make the slow descent to a flat outcropping just below the ten-thousand-foot marker. Thankfully, gravity did most of the work. Two hours later, in a shower of blowing snow and rotor-wash, it was up and away to safety.

The Cloud Peak climb had drained the last of the group's energy by the time they got back to their motel.

With Matt Grimes resting comfortably in the tender care of his new admirer in his hospital bed across town, the rest of the climbing team gathered in one motel room for the beer and pizza celebration of another peak bagged and the log entries recorded. They were half-assed watching an early season football game when the broadcast was interrupted. The screen screeched out a buzzing gray sound before turning to a rogue TV transmission.

"Hey man, get a load of this terrorist type dude in black pajamas and face mask. He's declaring jihad against the Great Satan. He says he has taken hostages and is threatening to execute someone on live TV."

"Holy Shit!" someone blurted out.

"Where's AC?" asked another.

"He's in the shower."

"Go get him."

The messenger knocked on the door, reluctant to interrupt the man, enjoying some relief from his cold night on the mountain. "AC, you better come see this, quick."

AC stumbled from the shower, still wrapped in his towel. "What, what is it now guys? Can't even wipe my ass without ..." pausing mid-sentence as he observed the image on the TV.

Five minutes after the messianic broadcast ended, AC got a call from his commander.

"Major Collins, you have been re-assigned to a special NSA/Homeland Security command center being set up in Yellowstone National Park. You will receive your instructions when you arrive. A Heli-transport will pick you up within the hour. Bring your climbing gear, all of it. And the peak baggers' gear, too."

"Sir?"

"Just do it, AC. This comes from way above my pay grade."

Ten thousand miles away from Yellowstone, a SEAL Team was fighting its way out of a botched snatch and grab operation. The last operation before returning stateside, it was supposed to be a milk run.

The plan had been to fast-rope a four-man team from an MH-60 Blackhawk helicopter into hostile territory a couple miles outside a Sunni village. The Blackhawk, an Army asset from the 160th Special Operations Aviation Regiment (SOAR) is specifically designed for special ops and can easily carry the insertion team and any extra Sunni passenger collected. They were to quietly infiltrate a lightly secured compound and grab a double agent informer who had been compromising American field operations. It all went sour only moments into the operation.

Fluid, real-time intel was coming into the SEAL Team compound HQ from informants imbedded near the target drop site. It started with three green light to go alerts, only to stand down each time to decipher new info. Frustrated, SEALS could only sit by patiently checking and rechecking their gear, waiting for the call.

The SEAL Team was comprised of four men: Toad Rawlings, group leader, HK sniper rifle. John "Jonsey" Walsh, Cincinnati, Ohio, communications, MK-48 machine gun. Terrence Bonnier "T-Bone" Jenkins, Savannah, Ga., medic, M-4 with the grenade launcher. And Earl "Big Earl" Johnson, Lubbock, Texas, navigator, non-standard M-60 heavy machine gun.

"Hey, T-Bone, what's up with rubbin' that worn out old coin hangin' 'round your neck? You've been wearing that thing since BUDS," poked Big Earl.

"Been carrying this with me since my Granddaddy died. He got it from his Daddy, and down the family since his Daddy's time. This lucky charm got all of us Jenkins through every war since the Civil War. My great, great, granddaddy was a freedman fightin' for the Union, for the 54th Massachusetts. Can't never have enough good luck in this business we're in."

Standing six feet, six inches and weighing 245 pounds, Big Earl patted his M-60 machine gun, and smiled. "Me and the big dog, we make our own luck."

Jonsey threw in his two cents' worth, "That old dinosaur? Armory Requisition's gonna tag your ass for all that ammo when we debrief."

"Dime for a dollar. Big 60 don't take no shit."

Toad nodded toward their bird, its rotor slowly coming up to operational speed. "Shake it, boys."

Finally, the call to lock and load came from HQ. Using normal insertion protocol, the MH-60 pilot flew a twisting turning path avoiding towns and villages in route, to avoid detection and deny the enemy random shots of opportunity. Each SEAL Team member made final gear checks, T-Bone rubbing his coin; Big Earl gently rocking to whatever tune was playing in his headphones. Nearing the target village, the pilot made three touch and go feints at different landing sites before dropping his payload, hopefully confusing an enemy as to the precise insertion point, preserving the element of surprise.

All plans have a weak point. The Team's Sunni guide, the one with a nasty habit of picking his nose with his left hand while speaking, had sold them out and led them into a trap.

Automatic weapons fire surrounded the SEAL Team when they hit the ground in the pre-dawn light. A quiet in and out mission became a fight for survival, and sunrise found the SEAL Team pinched on three sides with only one way out through a narrow pass: a sure and final ambush.

With incoming fire becoming heavier and more accurate, Toad keyed his mike.

"Defensive positions. T-Bone left flank. Jonsey, right flank. Earl, you hold the center. Do not let them advance on our position. Jonsey, call in fire support. Y'all hold 'em off 'till that Apache gets here. And keep your heads down."

T-Bone leaned back into the shelter of a covering bolder. Stacking spare magazines for his HK MP4N-9 machine gun, he mumbled to himself, "You got dat right."

To T-Bone's right, Big Earl planted the M-60's fold down bipod on a convenient boulder and snuggled the buttstock tight into his shoulder, challenging the enemy, "Come git some."

Five minutes is an eternity in a firefight.

The outnumbered SEAL Team, through select, concentrated firepower, was holding their ground against the Arabs' random, scattered barrages of light arms, AK-47s, and rocket-propelled grenades. The hide behind the rock, shooting with rifle held overhead, Allah guide my bullets' theorem was disproportionately ineffective, given their superior numbers.

In a lull in the gunfire and hunkered down behind his own sheltering boulder, Toad reached into a side pocket to retrieve a strange keepsake for a hard ass SEAL to carry into combat; the photo of AC, Christie, and himself taken at an amusement park two years earlier.

When another RPG round landed too close, Toad hollering to no one in particular, snarled "Yup, he's got my back alright." He stuffed the picture back into his wallet and spit a stream of tobacco juice in bitter contempt. Thoughts of home and his friends faded away as fast as the spittle drained away into the dry desert sands.

"Where's that damn Apache?"

Toad spied a goat trail winding up and over a shear wall at their backs and had an idea. "Listen up, guys. At the rate incoming is closing in on us, we don't have time to wait for the Apache. We got to take the fight to them. Cover me. I'm going for position."

The rest of the SEAL Team opened up with all they had, hosing the surrounding hillsides with automatic fire. Big Earl's '60 was "chewing the bone" in short staccato bursts; whump, whump, whump, its signature muzzle report claiming his 60-degree radius of fire; whump, whump; some rounds taking out multiple enemy dumb enough to advance in line; whump, whump, whump, whump, whump; Big Earl rocking with the '60's recoil, engaging multiple targets, much as he would in an arcade video game.

Darting from rock to rock like a sprayed cockroach, Toad made it to the top of the ridge amidst a withering hail of gunfire, splattering him with shrapnel shards of splintered rock and the ricocheting smell of cooking lead.

"Sons-a-bitches!"

Taking a position giving him a clear view of the battlefield, Toad began directing rifle launched grenade fire into the enemy positions that were blind to him from down in the gully.

"T-Bone, drop one behind that line of brush, 20 degrees left, eighty meters."

"Again, five degrees left. Bingo!" A couple of twitching pajama legs splayed out from behind a rocky outcropping confirmed a direct hit.

Using his glasses to pinpoint and range targets for his team's return fire was paying big dividends. Then he saw a familiar figure directing the enemy fire into his position.

"That damned guide. I'll fix that crap right now!"

Toad settled into a prone firing position with bullets whining past him like a swarm of angry hornets. He placed the sight reticle of his sniper rifle dead center, chin high on his turban wearing adversary. Six hundred meters, no windage, breathe, squeeze, BANG.

"Popped that nose picker!" The target crumpled to his knees and tumbled off his perch.

With their leader down, enemy courage and coordination began to falter. Toad ordered his men to advance under cover of his sniper fire. Every jihadist head popping up for a quick peek and shoot got a bullet for his trouble. At the sound of an incoming Apache, the opposition faded away, leaving twenty dead in their wake.

"Ground Forces Commander, this is Wizard, five miles out."

'Bout time you got here." Toad's icy stare and steel toned voice leaving no doubt as to his meaning.

"Sorry, we got a little busy back there."

"Multiple hostiles on the run, zero-one-zero my position, 600 meters. Targets marked by our tracer fire. You are cleared weapons free. Follow 'em up and spank 'em hard, Wizard. Give 'em something to remember us by. We got it covered here. And call us in a ride home."

"Aye, Chief."

The Apache pulled away as Toad gathered his crew. The retreating sound of small arms fire and the mini gun reply gave testimony to the futility of direct engagement.

"Stand down. See to your gear, and Jonsey, you take watch 'till our ride gets here."

Big Earl fed a fresh bandolier of ammo into his weapon, its muzzle still smoking from the heated firefight. "Yep, dime for a dollar, and you can keep the change."

At the sound of the incoming MH-60 Blackhawk, "Toad" Rawlings waved toward the LZ. "Let's go home boys."

Twelve hours after debriefing, a cleaned and packed SEAL Team settled in for the long flight home when they got an urgent, secured phone call from Pentagon Operations.

"Master Chief Rawlings, special orders. You and your crew have been re-assigned. You're on a red eye flight to Washington."

"Sir?"

"This is no drill, Toad."

"You got to be shittin' me. My guys are beat. They've done nine missions back-to-back. They've earned some R and R."

"This is by direct order of the President. Lock and load, Master Chief."

Toad turned to his crew, making direct eye to eye contact with each man, "Roger, Sir."

CHAPTER 13: THE BLIND SIDE

Two terrible weeks had passed since the hay wagon arrived at an abandoned farmhouse deep in the woods on the Saskatchewan side of the Canadian border.

For two hours each day since their capture Dr. Ainslee was beaten and tortured by a man Kamal addressed as Assan, a smallish man with cold dark eyes, greasy black hair and the chiseled facial features of a rat clothed in a scraggly black beard. His ragged yellow teeth overfilled a permanent cruel snarl atop a receding weak chin. He spoke no English, so all questions and threats were proffered by Kamal Rashid.

The routine was the same each day, the object of the torture the same. Each session began from a different reference point, as if the probing from different angles would guarantee a consistent result.

It started with a brutal beating of the helpless Ainslee tied prostrate on the ground, kicking at his head and unprotected rib cage, booted blows to his crotch, and ears. As the blows fell, Private First-class George Ainslee retreated into a prior life, alternatively cursing his captors with muzzled grunts of "Mother Fuckers" and Marine Corps trained repetition of his name, rank, and serial number. The first round of beatings was followed by hog tying the man, belly down, hands tied behind him, his legs pulled up tight to his back and the rope tied around his neck. In this way, he had to strain between breaths to keep the tension from strangling him to death. And Assan watched on, almost orgasmic in his doling out of pain on his helpless victim.

The hopelessly tied Dr. Albright could only look on in horror, her cries for mercy falling on deaf ears.

At the point of passing out, Ainslee's ropes were loosened, then questioning and indoctrination began anew.

Kamal Rashid began in his polished Boston College English, "We are the soldiers of Allah. It is righteous and just that you tell us what we want to know. The Sword of Allah will soon smite the Great Satan. Tell me, infidel, where is the doorway to Yellowstone's molten heart?"

And on it went. The beatings, starvation rations, the degrading of self and inner willpower to endure, the dreaded anticipation of the next round of torture. The theme of each torture session remained the same. How to penetrate Yellowstone's labyrinth of caves, caverns, and lava tubes to reach its beating heart.

In the brief respite between beatings, Christie huddled over the tortured and beaten ghost of the man who had been Dr. George Ainslee lying semi-conscious upon a rotten pallet on the floor. Little better off than he, Christie nursed his pain with sips of water and kitchen scraps thrown their way.

The two prisoners kept their conversations mute to the ears of their captors, lest they invite even more kicking and beatings. Both had never been closer to their God than in these moments surrounded by godlessness manifested. Prayers were spoken eye to eye. Lips moving in silent unison held them in their faith, the inner flame burning in their hearts and minds, reciting the 23rd Psalm.

"The Lord is my Shepard; I shall not want. He maketh me to lie down in green pastures; he leadeth me beside the still waters. He restoreth my soul; he leadeth me in the paths of righteousness for his name's sake. Yea, though I walk through the valley of the shadow of death, I will fear no evil; for thou art with me; thy rod and thy staff, they comfort me. Thy preparest a table before me in the presence of mine enemies; thou anointest my head with oil; my cup runneth over. Surely goodness and mercy shall follow me all the days of my life; and I will dwell in the house of the Lord forever."

The central question of each torture session was the same. "Tell me again, where is the place I want to know. Where is the doorway to Yellowstone's molten heart?"

Kamal placed a geodetic survey map out before Dr. Ainslee.

The broken body of Dr. Ainslee kept hidden from Kamal the fierce spirit that even the Viet Cong could not break. He had heard in hushed whispers hints about some great plan to cripple America. He could not imagine what it might be. What could a terrorist want with an extinct lava tube? He would play the game to keep both himself and Christie alive long enough for some turn of fate to intervene, to thwart whatever kind of mayhem this Kamal was planning.

Finally, his energy and courage at an ebb, he spoke clearly, hoping the cauldron of molten lava would end the evil plan. "Dragon's Mouth is the place you seek, on a lava dome above the river, here," pointing to a spot on the map.

On a snowy September 10th, fifteen days after the kidnapping, six men and a captive in an ATV emerged from the forest with enough assault gear to fight a small war. They packed AK-47 assault rifles, bullet-proof vests, climbing gear, and something closely guarded and praised in their Pashtun gibberish as something special to Allah. They also had some high-tech communication gear and a satellite dish.

That something special had, in the month past, ridden a pack mule down from the Tora Bora mountains of Afghanistan, smuggled aboard a French registered freighter at the port of Karachi hidden in a crate of machine parts, and entered a port in Toronto, Canada by way of the St. Lawrence Seaway. A twenty-hour train ride on the Canadian Pacific Railroad and a short ATV ride delivered it and its nefarious shepherds only another four hours' distance from its final destination.

The Sword of Allah had dodged the watchful eye of Satan's army, whose attention was directed elsewhere.

Allah is truly great!

CHAPTER 14: ROAD TO MECCA

"WE GOT HIM!"

The long-awaited call came into Dan Shield's office at the Bureau Headquarters.

"Put it on speaker," Dan ordered. "Identify yourself."

"Coast Guard Petty Officer First Class Nunez, Sir. We just came back off patrolling sector seven and were readying to berth when our sonar got a ping from below the Bay Bridge. It's one of those mini-subs, Sir."

"You're sure about that?"

"No mistake, Sir. Sonar guys can hear his O2 generators running."

"How in hell did he make through our dragnet?"

"They're super secretive, almost invisible to track, Sir. How do you want me to handle it?"

"Can you raise him? I want this guy bad. Call for backup and keep this line open."

"Yes, Sir."

146

Agent Shields made a call to the White House. A hurried scrum of bureau chiefs, top brass and the President gathered around the intercom.

"Agent Shields, do you believe this to be the threat we've been throwing all these assets at for the last two weeks?" The President asked.

"That's our best intel, Mr. President. I grilled that Mustafa son of a bitch really hard. I think we may have won this round, Sir."

In the next thirty minutes, three United States Navy gunboats from the Bay Area Naval Station were on the scene around the main bridge abutment on the Frisco side of the Bay. Police blockades cleared traffic on both sides of the bridge and two city blocks in either direction. All boating and commercial traffic in and out of the Bay area was ordered to withdraw two nautical miles from the area under total radio communication blackout.

"Mr. President, we hailed the sub and got no response. But we can hear him starting his engines."

"Take him now. I want those bastards taken alive, if possible."

"Yes, Sir. Dropping depth charges near him now. We'll raise him, Sir."

Two dull, yellow flashes eighty feet below erupted in surface gushers.

Inside the crippled sub, its crew donned their martyr scarves and said a last prayer.

"She's coming up, Sir."

"Stand ready to board."

In the situation room back in Washington they watched this unfold on a live, secure video feed from helmet cams of sailors raising the sub.

The instant the blue and gray colored hull breached the surface, the command was given.

"Go, Go, Go!"

Two sailors trained their automatic weapons on the small conning tower of the sub, while a third prepared to pop the hatch.

Those in the Situation Room were all head nods and smiles in sure anticipation of a major terrorist take down.

The hatch screw began to turn. Sailor three had his weapon and head cam fixed on what happened next.

Slowly, the hatch began to rise. Another sailor grabbed the lid from behind the conning tower and yanked it backward. The head cam peered inward, straight into the cold black eyes of jihad and to the detonator in his hands.

With a half-smile and thumb press, the video went dead.

The black and orange blast crushed the hulls of the four Navy and Coast Guard boats, instantly killing everyone on board. The shock wave pulverized the very foundation of the Bay Bridge, and as seen on live national broadcast from a local news crew on the scene, the bridge buckled, swayed, and fell into the Bay in one mighty WHOOSH!

The Situation Room went silent. As shock slowly turned to reality, a "Code Red" call was forwarded from Homeland Security. The President nodded to the Secretary of Defense to put it on speaker.

"Sir. It's Al Qaeda taking credit for the Bay Bridge bombing."

The caller identifying himself as Kamal Rashid, spoke directly to FBI agent Dan Shields.

"Agent Shields, a thousand years of jihad has brought us to this day. I trust you enjoyed the wake-up call in San Francisco."

Speaking in apocalyptic terms, Kamal promised a worldwide broadcast of the death of The Great Satan on live TV September 11 at 1:00 p.m. Eastern Standard time. To secure his audience, Kamal taunted FBI agent Dan Shields, connecting the dots between the Boston Marathon bombing and the kidnapping of Yellowstone's Dr. George Ainslee and Dr. Christie Albright.

His guts in knotted anguish, Dan suppressed his emotions. "The hostages. Prove to me they're still alive. Let me speak to Dr. Albright."

"They are as Allah wills them to be. Yes, they will live to serve Allah. Know this, Agent Shields, and all the infidels awaiting Allah's justice; I will pave the road to Mecca with American blood."

The results of the bridge bombing were instant and spread outward as ripples on a pond. Traffic on both ends of the former bridge became snarled and impassible, so emergency vehicles could not reach victims.

Yerba Buena Island was cut off. Ferries could not travel directly between San Francisco and Emeryville. Power cables and water mains which ran under the bridge deck were severed, leaving thousands without utilities. Service vehicles, delivery trucks, shipping terminals, and air traffic came to a standstill. The bay was also one of the busiest waterways on the northern coast. Ships of all sizes, arriving and departing one of the most important sea terminals in the world, were forced to drop anchors, both around Alcatraz and seaside of the Golden Gate Bridge. Docks at terminals quickly became choked with cargo, and inbound ships still at sea were told to divert to other terminals.

The White House situation room went from stunned silence to chaos. Agencies such as FEMA. Homeland Security, Departments of Interior, Commerce,

Transportation, and Justice were all given orders from the President through cabinet level posts. The Joint Chiefs of the military were ordered to prepare to assist under a Temporary Action Order. The military had significant assets in California, but it would take time to organize.

Life in and around San Francisco would be disrupted for years to come.

CHAPTER 15: ARMAGEDDON

In full crisis mode, the heads of NSA, CIA, and Homeland Security gathered in the Situation Room at the appointed time. They knew this was no drill.

The big screen at the head of the conference table crackled to life at exactly 1:00 p.m. as promised. All the world watched in horror and disbelief.

A nervous anxiety permeated the room as a black shrouded figure walking with a slight limp came into focus. Behind him in a semi-circle were five other men similarly clothed in black military fatigues with a bright green arm band below the right shoulder: all brandishing AK-47 assault rifles and bandoliers of ammunition. Between them was a covered object roughly the size of a rucksack draped with an Al Qaeda battle flag. Christie Albright sat cross-legged and bound beside the speaker, while immediately before him knelt Dr. George Ainslee, blindfolded, and wearing an orange jumpsuit, his hands tied behind him.

The shrouded speaker began by tearing away his face covering and stared directly into the camera, one blind eye a shrunken, faded bluish orb, the other blood red hot with hate and rage.

"I am Kamal Rashid, the new face of jihad. Infidels, and non-believers, today is the day the battle of a thousand years is won. That, by the power and will of Allah, will once and for all wipe clean the paganism of the infidels. Al Qaeda takes its rightful place in world-wide jihad this day by bringing The Great Satan to its knees. We will leave your homeland a charred and dying wasteland, a reminder to all the world that our time has come. No more will you thwart the spread of Sharia to all the righteous people of the world. The West and its poisonous ways will be wiped clean starting here today, in the heartland of The Great Satan, Yellowstone National Park."

Kamal waved his arm toward the object under the flag, nodding to one of his mongrel pack to pull away the flag. To the knowing eye, what was revealed was trouble, really bad trouble. Long rumored, but never actually seen before, sat a device looking like the top-secret description of a Russian backpack Thermo-nuclear bomb.

"See with your own eyes the instrument of your destruction. The Sword of Allah will smite the infidels from his mountain fortress, to turn loose the fury of Yellowstone's volcano such has not happened in 600,000 years. You cannot run, you cannot hide. The deed is already done. This broadcast has been delayed by several hours, enough time that we have already descended into the earth, to the heart of Yellowstone. You cannot stop us. It is already too late.

"Run, cry out to your false God. See that he cannot help you. There is only one true God, praise Allah.

152

"To know that my words are true, see this infidel before you."

Kamal ripped away the blindfold from Dr. Ainslee's eyes. His bruised and blackened face was briskly shoved only inches from the camera.

"Speak your last words, infidel. Confess your sins and beg for Allah's mercy."

Undefeated eyes looked directly into the soul of everyone present in the Situation Room. They all knew what was coming next. Some were transfixed. Others wanted to turn away but could not.

Agent Shields cursed under his breath, knowing that he had taken Abdoul Mustafa's baited story and misdirected all those resources on a feint.

Abdoul Mustafa's place in Mecca was assured.

"I've been chasing the wrong dog all this time. Damn those raggedy assed bastards. Damn Kamal Rashid!"

George Ainslee began numbly reciting the forced confession about the world-wide oppression of Muslims by the West, and the saving grace of Allah. He knew he was about to die. At the end of Kamal's scripted rant, the once Private First-Class George Ainslee, United States Marine Corps, focused on the little red blinking light on the camera, and with his last breath forcefully declared —

"Semper fidelis, os dracones."

Thinking that to be some last heathen prayer, Kamal let it pass unedited, then suddenly jerked back his prisoner's head, and severed it with a single stroke of a long, curved blade.

Kamal held the severed head before the camera and shouted to the accompaniment of his brother jihadists,

"Death to America, Death to The Great Satan. Allahu Akbar."

Celebratory gunfire and shouts of Allahu Akbar reverberated in the streets of Islamabad.

Christie Albright lay shocked and quivering on the ground.

The video went viral. World-wide panic ensued.

The White House Situation Room went quiet, save for the retching sound of a stenographer vomiting in a corner trash can.

"Mr. President?" The Secretary of Defense, his ashen face pale from seeing such a horrid act, addressed his Commander-in-Chief. "Your orders, sir?"

The President, trembling with anger and incredulity, gathered his thoughts. "Get me the head of the United States Geological Services. I want to know all there is to know about Yellowstone."

"Get Special Forces on standby, too."

"Which ones, Sir?"

"All of them, damn it! No, countermand that. Get me SEAL Team Six. They dusted those mother fu—"

"Sir?"

"Just get me SEAL Team Six."

"I want that film dissected frame by frame. Tell me we got something to work with here. NSA, can you trace that broadcast to its source?"

"Get me somebody to analyze that bomb."

"And what's with that horseshit green arm band he's wearing?"

"I want an action report back here in one hour."

"And get me Dan Shields. Pronto."

CHAPTER 16: SEAL TEAM SIX

The crisis at Yellowstone went viral around the world. The stock market crashed and closed. Thousands of tourists in Yellowstone National Park were fleeing for their lives. Jackson Hole and nearby mountain communities became like ghost towns. The interstates became jammed with thousands upon thousands, trying to get as far away from the epicenter of the pending blast as possible. Snow covered highways were reduced to single lane traffic littered with stranded vehicles man-pushed out of the way by those still able to negotiate the carnage. Some, knowing instinctively that running as far and as fast as they might, they would not escape the thousand-mile radius death cone of a Yellowstone eruption. Others simply sat and waited in a prophetic End of Days stupor. Airports ground to a standstill. Terrified passengers, rioted to get onto grounded planes, overwhelmed a disoriented security force trying to catch a terrorist wind that had long since blown through.

Doom's day prophets and survivalist groups took shelter in underground bunkers, while churches were overfilled with those making the frantic search for last-minute salvation. There was also rioting in the streets of every major city in America. Martial Law was enacted nation-wide to stem the rampant looting and lawlessness by those who were off the chain to do as they pleased without threat of reprisal or punishment.

The once almighty Great Satan became impotent, resigned. Allah must surely have been pleased.

The Situation Room at the White House reconvened what had been named Operation Brimstone.

Dr. Brian Hodges, head of the USGS, brought up a computerized display of the Yellowstone caldera and its historic eruption patterns on the large video screen.

"The magma chamber beneath Yellowstone is pressurized to thirty-six thousand atmospheres, or five hundred twenty-nine thousand pounds per square inch. In a worst-case scenario, an eruption would have the same catastrophic affect as a major nuclear strike. The explosion of Yellowstone would displace enormous volumes of air with massive shock waves which would be felt across all of America, Canada, and Mexico.

"For example, an air pressure of two atmospheres would affect balance and hearing. A few more would induce an instant case of the bends such as that which deep-sea divers encounter. Air pressures we could expect from a

Yellowstone blast would flatten forests, and anything else in its path. Vaporized rock would create a blast of heat like one hundred mile per hour flame throwers incinerating everything. I'm talking complete annihilation of everyone and everything within a thousand-mile radius of the eruption. Post explosion, the displaced atmosphere would rush back into the void like a second, high explosive detonation. We would be hit with a double whammy. What doesn't get destroyed by the initial blast will be destroyed by the incoming back rush of air.

"Climate disruption world-wide would be inevitable. We would enter a nuclear winter. Air and water pollution world-wide, failed crops, and mass starvation would follow. The explosion of a super volcano like Yellowstone could trigger a major extinction event."

The big screen showed the growing plume of destruction spreading across the Midwest, smothering Chicago, and blanketing the East coast under a suffocating crust of ash and brimstone.

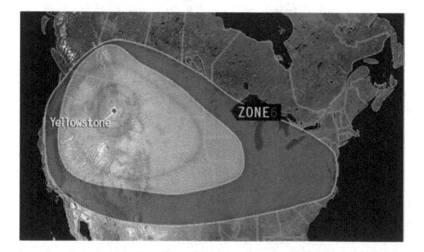

A great sucking sound of quiet disbelief settled the room.

"If Yellowstone blows," Dr. Hodges continued, "you can stick your head between your legs and kiss your ass goodbye. Recovery time would be measured in hundreds of years. In other words, lights out, game over, the end of North American civilization as we know it."

The President turned to Agent Shields who slipped into the room during the presentation.

"Dan, you've been tracking this Kamal character since the Boston bombing. You know how he thinks. Yellowstone National Park is huge. Where do we start to look for this guy, and how much time do we have? Can he really pull this off, and what can we do about it?"

"Mr. President, as you know, this kind of national sabotage has been a long time coming. The international problem of radical Islam has been showering the sparks of anarchy around the globe like a windblown campfire setting the woods ablaze. Something like this was inevitably bound to come at us from across our very borders with Canada or Mexico.

"The Muslim population of Canada, particularly eastern Canada, has grown from thirty-three thousand in 1971 to over a million today. There are almost half a million Muslims living in Toronto alone, and a high majority of them are Pakistani. Even at the odds of one radicalized jihadist in every thousand immigrants, we are looking at 500 bad actors, and Sir, this Kamal is the worst of the worst.

"That bright green arm band they were wearing represents an ancient Arabic cult going back to the Quran, (Surah 18:31). Green paradise, or something like that, awaits all true believers. These guys are committed."

A CIA analyst spoke up. "Mr. President, my guys have analyzed the footage we just reviewed and they're fairly sure Kamal has the real thing. They are holdovers from the Cold War, and they are real indeed."

A clerk motioned to Dan Shields.

"Sir, we just got this from the stenographer in this morning's meeting."

"You're talking about the one who puked in the President's trash can?"

"Yes, sir. She has a background in Latin studies, and she picked up on something in the video that we missed."

Dan Shield studied the note.

"Mr. President, it looks like we have a lead on where Kamal plans to detonate that bomb. Dr. Ainslee slipped it into his Semper Fi farewell. Os Dracones, loosely translated from Latin, means Dragon's Mouth. It's an ancient lava tube created by Yellowstone's last eruption."

The President responded, "That was one tough son of a bitch. Must be true what they say, once a Marine always a Marine."

"CIA has confirmed that the Russian KGB had plans to smuggle miniaturized nuclear devices into America and hide them in sensitive targets to be simultaneously detonated in the event of open war between the two superpowers, giving them a crippling, confusing first strike strategic advantage. The United States and the Israelis both have similar weapons. We have our MK-54 special Atomic Demolition Munition (SADM), the Russians have their RA-115."

"RA-115?"

"Yes, Mr. President. The RA-115 was intended to be operated by Soviet SPETZNAZ, their special forces. The existence of these weapons has been classified Top Secret and has never been publicly acknowledged.

These weapons are everyone's boogie man in the closet. They are easily concealed, easily transported, and have enough bang to do some real damage. Many of them have been unaccounted for since their existence was disclosed several years ago."

The President addressed Shields and the group in the Situation Room. "What are we talking about here? I mean, how much damage can a single backpack bomb do?"

The CIA analyst explained. "Mr. President, Osama bin Laden bought some of these weapons from Chechen rebels who pilfered them from abandoned Russian military compounds when the Russian empire crashed back in the '80s'. NSA heard they paid thirty-six-million dollars for as many as twenty of these things. It's feared Al Qaeda scientists have devised a way to hot wire the bombs to martyrs who would carry them to chosen targets."

"The RA-115 is relatively light weight of about sixty pounds, with an explosive yield of two kilotons; enough to take out an entire New Your City block. On the battlefield they could be used to take out critical infrastructure, shape the battlefield terrain, collapse a mountain, use your imagination. It's a lightweight compared to the Hiroshima bomb of sixteen kilotons. They were intended to be tactical nuclear weapons of medium yield. In this scenario they would act as the blasting cap to set off a much larger event. According to our USGS expert here, plenty sufficient to do the job of fracturing the caldera outer wall, creating a magma tsunami beneath Yellowstone."

"This monster hasn't been unleashed in almost 600,000 years and is long overdue for another eruption. All it needs is a precisely placed nudge. Two kilotons would be that nudge, Sir."

"Why can't Kamal just drop the damn thing into one of those lava tubes from the surface with a timer?" the President asked.

"Not so simple." USGS Brian Hodges directed all eyes to the big screen, bringing up a map of Yellowstone.

I understand the backpack devices are designed to be safe and stable to allow for the rigors of transportation. They must be placed at their destination before they can be armed to detonate. The underground passageways of Yellowstone would be an exceedingly difficult descent, even for professionals. It is not a straight line to the heart of the volcano. It could take a couple of days to navigate the descent of several miles in extreme conditions. Hell, it takes a week to climb Everest IN THE DAYLIGHT. The terrorists have to get this thing into the magma chamber to cause enough seismic pressure to induce the eruption.

Dr. Ainslee may have been a bit eccentric, but he knew his geology. While using ground penetrating sonar for routine monitoring of the volcano, he also mapped the underground labyrinth of lava tubes and caverns beneath the park.

Using his pointer, Hodges overlaid a map of Dr. Ainslee's underground charts onto the Yellowstone map.

"All the gas vents, hot pools, boiling sulfur pits and lava tubes originated from past volcanic activity, and they all trace back to the same source. Some are deathtraps, some might be navigable. Looking at his charts, it looks to me like Dr. Ainslee gave your Kamal the longest route possible at the Dragon's Mouth. If you were to insert your SEALS here, pointing to a fissure in the Fire River drainage ten miles away from the Dragon's Mouth, your guys just might have a chance to cut Kamal's lead in half."

The President turned to the CIA analyst.

"How much time do we have?"

"If that bomb is the real deal, and if Kamal can get it far enough into the volcano to trigger an eruption, I'd say no more than twenty-four hours, Sir."

Shields turned to newly arrived SEAL Team Leader, 'Toad' Rawlings. A vague familiarity prodded his memory.

"Have we met before?" he asked.

"I don't think so, Sir. I've been eating rocks and sand in some gosh awful places for the last two years. I just arrived from an overseas op. DOD gave me a short briefing on the flight here. Hardly had the chance to change my drawers yet, Sir."

"Anyway," Shields said. "What do you think about breaking up into two teams? One follows Kamal from the Dragon's Mouth, maybe catching him from behind or at least blocking his retreat. The other team goes in at Fire River, hoping to get ahead of him."

Toad turned to Dr. Hodges.

"What if Kamal detonates that thing when we catch him? He knows his plan is a one-way suicide gig. I mean, even for a crazy rag-head, dead is dead, ain't it?"

"You ever play with firecrackers as a kid?" Hodges asked.

"Yeah, I got caught dropping M-80 firecrackers into the locker room toilets in high school. Blew those suckers right off the floor!"

"Well, for Kamal to get this far, I'm betting he's done his homework. He knows a premature detonation will only make a sloppy mess. To get the job done right, he must get that bomb all the way down to the magma chamber wall. Anything less is a firecracker in a toilet."

"Sounds like a plan to me," Toad replied.

"That's it then." Turning to the President, Dan Shields offered; "With your permission, Sir, I'll work with Homeland Security to set up an Operations Center at both the Dragon's Mouth and Fire River.

"Master Chief Rawlings, you insert half your guys, we'll call Team Alpha, at the Dragon's Mouth. I'll go in with Team 'Bravo' at Fire River. We'll catch Kamal in a crossfire and put his lights out before he can get that bomb far enough into the volcano to set it off."

Sir, you're a civilian. It's going to be hot beyond belief and we'll all have to wear respirators to protect against the noxious gasses certain to be there. You sure you want to do this? I've told my guys to get right with their families and get right with God. This one might be a one-way trip."

"Master Chief Rawlings, I appreciate your concerns, but this is personal. Kamal Rashid started this a long time ago in my hometown. I aim to finish it right here, right now, in Yellowstone."

The President looked both men in the eyes, knowing full well what he was asking of them. He nodded his approval. "Good luck, gentlemen, and God's speed! The Nation's prayers are with you."

CHAPTER 17: THE BELLY OF THE BEAST

W hen the SEAL Team's full complement of twelve men and two CH-47 Chinook helicopters got to the Dragon's Mouth, they found a complete mobile operations center, communications gear, generators, aid station and supplies already on site by way of Homeland Security. Touch down covered everything in a swirling blanket of snow.

A Navy demolitions expert was also on the scene to disarm the RA-115 if they stop Kamal in time. And they found one other asset not listed on their manifest, just flown in from Cloud Peak, Wyoming.

Standing beside a pile of climbing gear, with his back turned against the chopper's rotor wash, was a lean, angular figure instantly recognized by Master Chief Rawlings.

First out of the lead aircraft and followed by Dan Shields, Toad Rawlings rushed to confront Major AC Collins. Grabbing AC by the shoulder and spinning him around, Toad pushed up into AC's face and barked, "No fuckin' way this jarhead washout is on my team!"

AC pushed back. "Toad, you couldn't find your ass in the dark with both hands."

Instantly taking a dislike to the unwelcome confrontation, Dan Shields shoved himself between the two men.

"Get your shit together! Our immediate problem is larger than whatever pissing match is going on between you two. Defense says Major Collins has the SEAL training your guys have, and the climbing skills they don't. Fast roping from a helicopter into a hot LZ ain't the same as climbing three miles down into the belly of a goddamned volcano. We got no time for this horse shit. Save it for Kamal. We have to make up this operation as we go along, and Collins here already has the specialist gear we need to get underground. So, get over it, and get on with it. Understood?"

Dan began prepping his gear and thinking back to the picture he saw in Christie's apartment. "Now I know where I've seen these two guys," he mumbled.

Looking over his shoulder toward Toad and AC, he barked, "You two would do well to remember that Kamal has your Christie Albright held hostage. Your fight is with him, not each other."

Like two junkyard dogs growling cheek to jowl, AC and Toad reluctantly backed off.

AC got everyone into their climbing harnesses and explained the rappel down into the volcano.

Master Chief Rawlings separated his SEALS into two six-man teams, counting off the squad members to go to Fire River with Dan Shields and AC, and those going with him to Dragon's Mouth. Each SEAL carried self-energizing night vision goggles, an air breather to filter out noxious gases they may encounter, the SEAL favorite HK MP5N 9mm sub-machine gun, fighting knife, and 9mm Glock sidearm.

Each team carried enough rations and water for two days. Any longer than that, and they wouldn't need it, anyway.

As Team 'Bravo' turned to board its Chinook headed for the Fire River command center, Toad called out to AC.

"I'll see you in Hell, jarhead."

AC fired back, "That's the plan, squid."

Team 'Bravo' flew off toward Fire River as Toad's Alpha team prepared for its descent into the Dragon's Mouth vent tube.

Meanwhile, in the Situation Room in Washington, the President asked the NSA technician, "Have you gotten a trace on Kamal's transmission?"

"The interdiction team is already airborne, Sir."

A combined CIA/Delta Force team secured the location at the farmhouse where Dr. Ainslee and Dr. Albright were held hostage and began a forensic examination of the premises. Their report, on a secure line, was simultaneously piped to the White House Situation Room and both SEAL Teams at Dragon's Mouth and Fire River. It confirmed the presence of trace amounts of PU239, a radioactive residue from the Russian nuclear device.

"Mr. President, it's the real thing," reported the team leader. "The threat is real. And Sir, we found Dr. Ainslee's body."

"Anything else?"

"Yes Sir. We found Dr. Albright's driver's license, and a note to Dan Shields."

"Read it."

"FBI Agent Dan Shields.

If you have found this note, you know it is too late to stop me. Allah and Osama bin Ladin will have their revenge, and I will have my reward. Your Christie Albright will be the first of my seventy virgins in heaven. If you try to follow me, she will go without her head."

The radio at Fire River and the Dragon's Mouth crackled to life, instantly dismissing old grudges with that news.

"AC, d'you get all that?"

"Yeah Toad, we got it."

"This dragon ain't got nothin' on us, Brother. We got some work to do."

"Toad, you paint 'em and I'll bust 'em. Meet you in the middle."

"Roger that."

The Dragon's Mouth vent had been silent for almost six hundred thousand years. Geologic wear and tear of the ages partially filled its entrance with fractured boulders and a jungle of brush. It had been marked Off Limits to tourists and hikers since the Park opened, and had never been explored, only charted sonically by Dr. Ainslee.

Homeland Security did a fair enough job of clearing out brush and rubble to allow Toad's SEAL Team room to rappel single file. It was apparent though that they were not the first to attempt the effort. Still fresh brush cuttings dusted with snow vetted a single half-assed rigging tied around a boulder, its far end stretching somewhere far below.

Kamal!

As no flashlight could penetrate the Stygian blackness, the SEALS would rely solely on Dr. Ainslee's charts, and their night vision goggles to navigate the volcano's underground passages.

Communication with the outside world had to be through a backpack spool of thin fiber optic line played out behind the SEAL Team, because no radio wave could escape the tortured passages underground. Man-to-man SEAL Team radios would still work at short line of sight distances.

Never one to lead from the rear, Master Chief 'Toad' Rawlings' was the first man in. He snapped a fluorescent green chem-light and tossed it into the void. Down, down, down it went until winking out of sight somewhere far below. Toad was about to drop over the lip of the vent mouth when a rushing roar from below became a virtual tornado of swirling bats running from the green light dropped into their daytime roost. Toad lost his balance and pitched headfirst into the darkness, saved only by AC's rigged harness. The rope made a singing sound, zzzzzzZZZZZzzzzzzz, as it raced through the turnbuckle, jerking him to a stop fifty feet below.

A loud "holy shit" echoed from the dizzying gloom of the lava tunnel.

"Toad, you alright?" hollered one of his team.

"Yeah, I'm OK. 'Bout shit my britches though."

Once inside the crowded mouth of the vent, it opened into a vertical shaft about thirty meters in diameter. According to Ainslee's chart, it had an initial vertical drop of about one hundred meters before making a more horizontal sloping angle towards a labyrinth of larger caverns and vent tubes, all headed toward Yellowstone's molten heart.

Toad finally touched down and lit another chem-light as a target for his men to follow. "Proceed, single file."

Ten minutes later the rest of 'Alpha' team and the Navy demolitions tech were assembled on the floor of the vent tube, checking gear, and studying Dr. Ainslee's charts.

Around them, scattered about the floor of the tube, were the fossilized bones of other animals that had fallen into the pit over the millennia, piles of buffalo carcasses, a giant ground sloth, and the dagger toothed skulls of Saber-tooth cats.

And one very recent addition to the bone yard; a dead Arab impaled on a stalagmite.

"Guess these desert rat bastards don't do much climbing, do they Chief?" quipped one of the team.

"Bats got him," added another.

"That's what I call stickin' to the job," came a third.

"That could have been you, Toad. Good thing Major Collins brought us this gear, huh?"

Toad spat a tobacco chaw into the dust.

"Everybody, tie off in ten-foot increments. Joe, you establish the comm link with command, topside. Earl, you repack the climbing gear. We're sure to need it. Keep in voice comm with us and get a hustle on. The rest of you, move out."

Toad, with four SEALS and the Navy demolitions tech, began trailing Kamal's footprints where visible in the dust and the bat guano on the floor of the vent. They had a small Geiger counter to follow minute traces of the Plutonium 239 trace radiation from the bomb.

Joe and Earl were packed and ready to catch up to the squad. Having left one climbing rig in place to get back to the surface, Earl turned and gave Kamal's rope a departing yank.

"Joe, would you look at this piece of sh—"

Topside of the vent shaft, Kamal's hidden IED was triggered by the terrorist's knowledge of human nature. It was inevitable that someone would be unable to resist a tug. BOOM! Shrapnel and splintered rock shards eviscerated the Dragon's Mouth communication command center. Bodies were vaporized, hardware incinerated, the whole mountain side collapsed over the mouth of the vent.

Down below, the blast force funneled through the narrow vent tube at supersonic speed. Joe and Earl were instantly vaporized into a pink misty dust. One hundred yards into the vent, and just beyond a forty-five-degree angled bend, the rest of the SEAL team was flattened by the blast.

Two miles and a half a day ahead of SEAL Team Alpha, Kamal heard the rumble of the blast and smiled. "The infidels. Allah be praised."

The Fire River Bravo team heard it, too: a long, drawn-out moan like the rumble of a distant thunderstorm. They could feel it through their feet.

Then they heard it again, coming back from the opposite direction. Was that an echo or an answering challenge from the Beast below?

The White House Situation Room made a call to Fire River.

"Agent Shields, come in."

"This is Shields."

"Dan, we lost Team Alpha. Toad's gone, all of them, gone. The command center, too. Sons 'a bitches rigged an

IED at the vent entrance. Brought the whole damn mountain down on top of them."

Agent Shields turned to AC and gave him the bad news.

The man was hard hit. Flushed with anger and emotion, AC turned to the blackness falling away before them and screamed into the void.

"RONNIE!"

Even the tough as nails SEALS dropped their eyes in a moment of respect for their fallen comrades.

From the Situation Room back in Washington, "Agent Shields, you and your team are our last chance to stop this thing. Get it done."

Twelve hours earlier Kamal's six-man terror squad, with hostage Christie Albright in tow, emerged from snowy anonymity, crossing the Canadian border six hours ahead of his delayed broadcast to America, and the tumult it would unleash. A brief rendezvous with an accomplice on the United States side of the border made the exchange from four-wheeler to Chevy van. When they approached the North Park Entrance, they were challenged by a park ranger on routine patrol.

"Hold up there, fellows. Park hours are 7:00 a.m. to 6:00 p.m. You'll have to wait 'till then. There's a breakfast place a couple miles back up the road. Go get yourselves something to eat. The gate should be open when you get done."

The ranger then noticed a scared looking female, her face partially covered in the back of the SUV. Something wasn't quite right with the situation.

With his left hand outstretched directly toward the van's driver, he commanded, "Hold on there."

The ranger walked back to his patrol car, reaching through the window for his radio, never taking his eyes off the idling Chevy. "Patrol, this is Ranger Huggins. I've stopped a suspicious vehicle, beige Chevy van, tag number AZH 147, at the North Park gate. Can you run a make on that tag ASAP?" Quickly confirming the SUV had been stolen, Ranger Huggins called for backup as he approached the SUV port side with his hand on his sidearm.

Nervous fingers clutching a hidden AK-47 and peering out from a rear window suddenly laced the park ranger and his patrol car with automatic fire.

Leaving the bullet ridden ranger prostrate in the roadway, his radio crackling orders to a dead man, the SUV rolled on.

Arriving at the entrance of The Dragon's Mouth a day in advance of his apocalyptic broadcast to the world and the SEAL Team's subsequent arrival, the under equipped Kamal Rashid began rigging rappelling gear to lower a first man to guide and cradle the descent of The Sword of Allah, followed by Christie, the others, and finally himself.

The first man had hardly begun to tie himself off when loose rocks around his feet gave way. He screamed for help, grasping at loose brush, searching the faces of his comrades with outstretched arms, then tumbled into the void, twisting, screaming, fading away into eternity. When an outgoing rush of black bats followed their comrade's death tumble, the other terrorists' jihad fervor melted into fear. Only at the barrel of Kamal's AK-47 did they submit to his commands to strap up and rappel into the darkness. Christie was given the choice of a free fall like the first man or using the rope. Kamal's last act in the outside world was to set the timer on a hidden IED to self-arm ten minutes after he was safely lowered into the lava vent.

Kamal's frightened group turned on their headlamps, looking around trying to get their bearings, when a head lamp light beam came to rest on the body of their lost comrade lying face up, dead eyes wide in terror, impaled on a glistening, runny, red mineral spike.

"Allah, be merciful."

Stunned by the blast from Kamal's IED, Toad Rawlings rose to his knees, trying to shake the spinning vertigo from his brain.

"Damn."

He rolled to his right side, then propped his back to the vent wall.

"Two arms, two legs, all hands and feet accounted for. Good to go!"

Looking around, he was relieved to see the rest of his team likewise trying to pull themselves together.

"Everybody Ok? Count it off."

Jonsey. "Aye."

Ed. "Aye."

Myles. "Aye."

"Joe and Earl didn't make it, Master Chief."

The remainder of the team reported in, except the Navy bomb tech. The last in line when the bomb blast engulfed them, he hadn't quite made it around the bend in the tunnel when the blast hit. The concussion slammed him into the wall, crushing him like a man stomps an empty beer can.

"Shit! Never even knew his name," one of the team remarked.

Toad rallied his team. "Gear check."

"Communication topside lost, Toad. It's sure we ain't goin' back that way."

"Well then, let's look at this as a tactical advantage. I'm sure that son of a bitch who dropped the mountain down on us thinks we're dead as last week's news, so he won't be expecting pursuit from behind. Stay sharp, stay ready. Let's go git some for Joe and Earl."

The Dragon's Mouth chamber echoed a defiant "HOO-YAH!"

One SEAL Team member commented, "Anybody else got that pounding in his head? Kinda sounds like listening to my own blood pressure pulsing in my ears on a cold still night, only louder."

His six o'clock answered, "That's not in your head. I hear it, too. It's coming from somewhere down there ahead of us."

Toad, pissed off, focused, and on the hunt, shouted "Cut the chatter. Move out."

The Fire River team "Bravo" had a much easier time of it. No huge vertical drops. No IED. They were making good time. With no way to track Kamal, they could only hope that Dr. Ainslee's charts were accurate, and they could reach the point where the Fire River tunnel met the Dragon's Mouth tunnel before Kamal got there. Holding to the premise that Kamal thinks he had cut off pursuit from the Dragon's Mouth, he had no idea he could still be thwarted from somewhere ahead of him. Advantage, Team Bravo.

AC called in a report topside to the Fire River command post.

"Making good time, footing is fairly smooth. The floor of this vent is like smooth peanut butter, but rock hard. It's dark and quiet as death down here, except for a low thumping sound, like a steam engine or pile driver miles away."

Fire River Command replied, "Nothing like that on our screens topside, Major."

Even though the mission to stop Kamal from blowing the lid off Yellowstone was life and death critical, with temperatures rising steadily as they descended, SEAL Team 'Alpha' had to stop every thirty minutes or so for a water and map orientation break. One misstep could be terminal.

One of the team members leaning against the vent wall rubbed the sweat from his face mask and pulled his hand back.

"What the hell is this?"

His face mask was covered in thick, black soot.

"Coal dust, dummy."

A quick look around revealed that the Fire River vent passed through a heavy vein of coal.

"What's coal doing way down here?"

"Dude, Wyoming is a major coal mining state. A zillion years ago all the West was a dinosaur swamp. Throw in a couple of million more years of heat and pressure and you got coal. Don't you ever read National Geographic?"

T-Bone spoke wisely; "Don't nobody light no matches."

"T-Bone, we've climbed half-way down to Hell and you're worried about a little fire?"

Dan Shields chimed in. "Cut the chatter. Break's over. AC, get 'em moving."

Three miles and half a day's trek into the bowels of Yellowstone, team 'Bravo' began to see a strange flickering glow ahead, like that of a dying light bulb. The walls of their lava vent widened into a great chamber that expanded upward and outward beyond their vision. A red and yellow light bouncing off crystalline walls was bright enough for them to take off their Night Optical Devices.

"Shields to Fire River command. You're not going to believe this, but we can see down here."

AC motioned to Dan Shields. "I guess we can get out of these harnesses from here on in."

"Everyone drop your climbing rigs in a pile and mark 'em with a green chem-light.

Unshouldering his gear, one man turned to his buddy, "This is some spooky shit, man."

"Yeah, and it's hot as three shades of Hell, too."

Like the red-hot glow of the blacksmith's forge, the molten heart of Yellowstone cast its eerie glow upward and into the cavern. Almost overpowering, its heartbeat, pulsing, thumping, roiling; the molten lava churning in the belly of the Beast, inhaling long cool droughts of top side air through long dead vents, its exhaling breath carrying a rhythmic blue and white static electricity arcing and spitting bolts of fire overhead.

One SEAL stretched his hand out to his buddies. "Look at this shit. My arm hair is standing straight up. Feels like ants crawling all over me."

Jonesy spoke up. "The 0-2 censor on my breather says we got good air down here!"

"Flick your Zippo. If she can breathe, so can we."

In the unworldly caverns below Yellowstone, SEAL Team Bravo, free of its encumbering climbing gear, night vision and air breathers, prepared for the 'morrow's battle.

In a lighter moment AC opined, "Boys, if we're gonna walk through the gates of Hell tomorrow, we might as well dine with the Devil tonight. Break it down. Night, day, it's all the same down here; however, we gotta get some rest. Pick a spot. T-Bone, you stand on point 'till Jonesy relieves you."

Like a campfire scene from an old western movie, Team Bravo settled around a pile of green chem-lights, small psychological comfort in an alternate reality that offered none. Munching packets of energy bars and drinking from camelback bladders, small talk echoed about the great chamber before them. For a few quiet hours, the SEALS of team Bravo allowed themselves to be just men.

"Man, I ain't never seen hot like this hot. That sweat down in the jungles of Panama last summer got nothin' on this place."

"Good thing this is supposed to be a two-day op. A goddam camel couldn't carry enough water to kill this thirst."

One hour on Dan Shields' watch was but a fleeting break from the thinly veiled anxiety each man felt about his role in the upcoming fight.

"Stand to. First punch wins the fight. Lock and load."

AC gathered Team Bravo into a huddle. "Listen up. Dr. Ainsley's chart has been right on the money so far. We entered the Fire River vent here. My AMBIT-3 watch says we are about three miles into the volcano which puts us here, pointing to a large void on the map. The Dragon's Mouth vent should be coming at us from about forty-five degrees to our left front. I'm guessing that hellacious roaring and pounding sound back to our right leads to the caldera. That has to be Kamal's target. Agreed?"

One of the team asked, "Major Collins, how do you want to proceed."

"Well, we can't just sit here and wait for him."

"Aye. Kamal's team could already be dead."

"Maybe so. But I've learned to never underestimate the survival skills of a rat. If I'm gonna be roasted alive down here, I'm for making sure that son of a bitch is done for, too."

"Roger that. We won't get a second chance at this."

Dan Shields offered; "If we get a hustle on, maybe we can get to the downside opening of the Dragon's Mouth vent before Kamal does. There we got a narrower field of fire to cover."

All heads nodded in agreement.

AC thought for a second. "Form a skirmish line, twenty-meter separation, and maintain voice comm."

The entire team responded as one, "Roger that."

A mile away and closing slowly, Kamal's team, unaccustomed to climbing, had underestimated the difficulty of their mission. They were thirsty and dehydrated to the point of exhaustion. Their Wal-Mart workshop protective masks did little to protect them from the Dragon's' breath. Theirs' would be a long night on the road to martyrdom.

Most distressed of all was Christie Albright, who had been made to carry the bomb, The Sword of Allah. She had sweated out, her unprotected face blistered from the intense heat, and her feet were bloodied knobs from the rough descent into the volcano. Willpower and Faith were her only allies. She would live only for as long as she could carry on.

"Kamal, why do you not let me kill her now," sneered Assan, tossing a feral look toward the exhausted woman. "She is of no further use to us. You have killed the Infidels who dared to follow us. She is a woman, a mule. My knife yearns for the taste of her blood."

Kamal rebuked his sergeant. "She represents all that I despise in the West, her pagan lifestyle, her arrogant sense of superiority. She and all her generations must pay for their sins. No, you may not kill her. I want her to know that she will be the first to witness Allah's victory. She will be tied to the bomb."

With a dismissive back hand to Assan, Kamal took a few steps away from his mongrel pack and pulled his prayer rug from his ruck sack. With no reference to East or West in Hell's Belly, Kamal simply began to pray. Reaching into a pocket, he clasped a dear object, a quiet tear weeping from his dead left eye. Even the coldest heart carries a spark of humanity. Kamal rose from his prayers and tossed a water bottle to Assan.

"Water the mule."

Assan mockingly dangled it inches from Christie's face, then twisted the top and took a long, deep swig. Ahhh. The rest he poured slowly into the sand at his feet.

Christie, her mouth too dry to spit, cut a look of defiance at Kamal as sharp as any knife, and hurled words from Revelations 16:13, "From out of the Dragon's Mouth come false prophets."

Taking no rest breaks for dead men, Toad Rawlings' SEALS had been steadily gaining on Kamal's suicide team. While Kamal had to feel his way along unfamiliar passages, SEAL Team 'Bravo' had only to follow the increasing register of their beeping Geiger counter.

Soon, Team Bravo could see a strange orange ambient light ahead of them. Untethered from their climbing rigs and discarded of their NODs and air breathers. Toad advanced his men, battle ready.

"That camel fucker can't be too far ahead now. I'm on point. Ed, Jonsey, you take the left flank. Myles, you take the right. Open mikes. Fire on contact. Don't take shit from these dudes."

Two hundred meters ahead of the fast moving 'Bravo' team, Christie stumbled and fell under the weight of the sixty-pound Sword of Allah. Assan began screaming and kicking her on the ground.

"Get up, get up, you infidel mule," he cursed, dragging Christie to her feet.

His bobbing headlamp drew an instant hail of gun fire from Toad Rawling's HK MP5. A hail of green tracer rounds vectored in from all sides.

One round caught Assan's left shoulder, spinning him to the ground. Another ricocheted off the shielded bomb on Christie's back, knocking her to the ground as well. Not knowing or caring who was shooting at her tormentors, Christie wriggled out of the bomb's shoulder harness and leapt behind a covering boulder. Assan dropped his AK and grabbed the bomb with his good arm, darting under a hail of fire toward his leader, taking cover behind a rock.

Christie, barely able to stand, rolled out from behind her rocky hide, grabbed the discarded AK, racked the bolt, and sprayed the retreating terrorists with splintering rock and lead.

Half a mile out into the open area of the cavern ahead of them, Team 'Alpha' was approaching the opening to the Dragon's Mouth lower vent when all hell broke loose ahead of them.

AC keyed his mike.

"Where's that firing coming from? Anybody see anything?"

"Nothing here."

"Then who—?"

The sporadic green and yellow tracers of a fierce firefight echoed and bounced around the cavern walls, the white-hot snapping of hot lead singing over their heads.

"I know the sound of that weapon. That's an HK."

A distant broken crackle came over AC's comm. "Ed, Jonsey, Myles, advance covering fire." Toad's men moved as a two-armed pincer to cover each other's flank, denying the enemy a single target for return fire.

"Pour it to 'em, boys," Toad ordered.

"Toad, is that you?"

"Who'd you think it was, jarhead?"

"Well, I was kinda hoping for Arnold Schwarzenegger, but I guess you'll do. You're supposed to be dead."

"Not yet, I ain't."

"Toad, I make you about 600 meters out. Kamal's got no clue we're ahead of him. Keep up the fire and drive him to us."

"Roger that, Brother. That piss-ant coward has some payback coming."

Kamal was running for his life, for his appointment with destiny. He and his two remaining terrorists were sprinting toward the distant glow and roar of the volcano's heart, now visible ahead of them when they were suddenly met with another wall of incoming HK fire.

Out in the world, Fire River command could hear what was going on below by way of the fiber optic communication line. On a relay to the Situation Room in Washington came the word; "Rawlings and Team Bravo are alive and back in the fight! They have Kamal in a cross-fire." Nervous hands wrung in helpless stress, some shouted, and fist pumped the air. All leaned forward in their chairs tuned to the speaker, eyes entranced by a vision of the life and death battle raging two thousand miles away in the bowels of Yellowstone.

Yellowstone's deep cavern was a maelstrom of gunfire and grenade explosions. Kamal's team made a stand, returning a voracious level of fire into both SEAL teams while shouting exhortations to Allah.

The very walls around the battlefield begin to shake, the hammering heartbeat of Yellowstone overwhelming all communications. Lightning bolts began to streak out of the furnace below in cracking, blinding flashes. They were literally fighting at the hot gates of Hell.

Toad yelled into his mike. "Damn AC, it's bad enough we got terrorists trying to kill us, without the volcano shooting lightning bolts at us, too."

Kamal, realizing that to stay and fight was to lose his chance at immortality, commanded his men to give him covering fire so he could detonate The Sword of Allah. He reached into a bullet torn pocket of the backpack to find that his remote triggering device had been destroyed.

Backed into a corner with no alternative and the courage of a trapped rat, Kamal shouldered the bomb and made a break for the inferno, his crippled leg no impediment to the call of martyrdom.

The retreating terrorists ran into the Team 'Alpha' firing line. Hand to hand combat ensued. Toad's Bravo team pushed the attack from behind.

One of the terrorists, assured of his soon trip to martyrdom, jumped up onto a ledge for better firing advantage hollering "Allahu Akbar." Toad turned to punch his ticket to paradise when the man was hit by a thundering lightning bolt from the volcano with the flash bang of a ground zero lighting strike. He disappeared in a puff of blue smoke like a mosquito in a backyard bug lamp.

The retreating Kamal, thinking he had beaten the SEAL Team firing line, ran face to face into Dan Shields.

They made eye contact.

Dan was first on the trigger, his Glock 23 pumping two close combat .40 caliber rounds center mass into Kamal's chest, dropping him face down in the dirt and slumped over The Sword of Allah. Forgoing a double tap head shot for fear of hitting the bomb, Dan's first instinct was to secure the RA-115. He grabbed a shoulder strap of the backpack to pull it free of Kamal's' body when the not so dead terrorist in a bullet-proof vest rolled over, shoving a pistol into Dan's face. An instinctive blocking forearm move deflected the shot away from his face and into his left shoulder, hurling Dan backwards.

Shrieking like a madman, Kamal grabbed The Sword of Allah and broke toward the roaring inferno.

AC arrived to help Dan to his feet when he got knocked stupid from behind with the rifle butt of the last terrorist's AK-47. The last of Kamal's men, Assan, shoulder wounded and with an ass sprayed limp from Christie's confiscated weapon, was about to execute Dan and AC when a green tracer bullet poked a third smoking eye in his forehead.

"Thanks for shooting that guy off me, Toad," shouted a grateful AC into his mike.

"Not me, Bro," Toad replied, pointing toward a boulder at his six o'clock.

Christie rose from her kneeling firing position fifty meters behind the fast-moving fire fight, fixing the now prostrate Assan squarely in her gun sights and giving him another parting round to carry with him to martyrdom. Giving the downed terrorist the one fingered salute, she hollered into the fiery abyss, "Not bad shootin' for a mule!"

Clutching the Sword of Allah, Kamal ran toward the inferno, leaping into a swirling static blue and white-hot vortex as old as the earth itself. The growing heat melted his Plexi-glass visor to his face, his air hose turned to liquid rubber, his skin crinkling and peeling like paint on a fire tossed piece of lumber in a campfire. The thing that was Kamal Rashid, now a flailing cinder, hurled himself and the nuclear bomb into the boiling caldera. Falling a vertical half-mile out of sight toward the glowing fire of Yellowstone's molten heart, Kamal screamed "Allahu Akbar" with his last breath in this world.

The rest of Team Alpha and Team Bravo gathered around AC and Dan.

AC shouted into his mike to overcome the roaring din of the inferno behind and below them. "Status check."

Team medic, T-Bone, cupped his mike, "Two wounded. None are life threatening. Dan took a clean round through the shoulder."

Hit with a sudden realization, Dan Shields spun around and shouted, "Christie! Shit, where's Christie?"

Then a voice, following up from behind them, called out.

"That's okay. Don't y'all worry about me. Shot, stomped, beaten, starved, boiled alive, and nearly blasted to Kingdom Come. But that's okay. Y'all just go on back slappin' each other. It's all okay."

She was hobbling along, using Assan's AK as a crutch.

Dan hurried to give her a supporting shoulder.

She turned to AC and Toad. "You boys sure know how to show a lady a good time. The last time I saw you two, you were tearing up that red neck bar in California."

Then the emotional wall that had kept her alive the last two weeks crumbled. She broke into tears, falling into Dan's embrace.

A sudden blue-white bolt of lightning crashed overhead and broke up the reunion.

One of the SEALS commented, "That fiery bitch don't like us being down here, does she?"

Gathering her composure, Christie couldn't restrain herself. "What makes you say my volcano is a fiery bitch?"

Toad threw a look over at the offending teammate, "Ever date a red head?"

In a moment of quiet reflection, AC studied the rocky gravel beneath his feet and casually stuffed a few volcanic stones into the pockets of his fatigues as keepsakes.

From deep below ground, Dan Shields broke the news to the President and the Situation Room.

"Mr. President, he got past us. I'm sorry Sir, there's no way to stop it now."

"How much time do we have?"

"Minutes, hours. No way to tell for sure, Sir."

CHAPTER 18: SEMPER FIDELIS

D an, get your people out of there."
Eighteen blistering hot hours later, a Medi-vac helicopter met the survivors at the mouth of the Fire River vent with orders to get them as far away from Yellowstone as possible. Retracing old ground climbing out of Yellowstone's subterranean labyrinth was quicker than going in. They were a beat-up bunch; three dead, two SEALS with thigh and shoulder wounds, Dan with a clean shot through the left shoulder, and Christie generally beat to hell, burned, and scalded. They were packed tight as sardines in a flying tin can with the medics bandaging wounds and pumping intravenous drips.

Toad's rage at having to back away from a fight boiled over.

"We lost three good men down there and now we just fly away and let that rat bastard Kamal take us down? That's all we got?"

An angry and frustrated Toad fired off an obscene rant vile enough to make a sailor cringe. "Mother fuckin' sons a' bitches."

Dan Shields, not straying too far from Christie's side, fired back at Toad.

"I want him as bad as you do, but he's toast, and we have hurt people here to attend to. Unless somebody's got a better idea, all your cussin' and spittin' is just white noise."

AC, jolted from deep thought, leaned toward Dan, and cupping his ear, asked, "What the fuck you sayin'?"

Hollering above the roar of the rotors, Dan yelled to AC.

"I told Toad to chop that noise! Crying about it won't change anything."

AC suddenly wheeled around toward the cockpit and grabbed the pilot by the shoulder, shouting into his headpiece.

"Turn us around. Take us back to Dr. Albright's lab in Yellowstone. I'll explain when we get on the ground."

The pilot looked to Shields, raising a questioning hand.

Dan turned to AC who mouthed the words, "Just do it," waiving the pilot onward.

Dan put in a call over the radio to the White House Situation Room.

"Mr. President, we have a plan. I don't know what it is yet, but Major Collins has re-routed us back to Yellowstone. Will report when we get there, Sir. Shields out."

The White House was buzzing with calls from around the world. Foreign markets were crashing. The Russians were getting itchy fingers. The incendiary rhetoric coming out of the Middle East threatened to boil over into Europe.

Every TV and news broadcast in America was on fire with fear and speculation about the fate of civilization.

The Reverend Franklin Graham, having just received the distressing news from his staff, segued from a previously scheduled 9/11 prayer vigil in the New York Giants football stadium. Fifty thousand attending souls inside the stadium, and millions more tuned to his national broadcast, clung to his every word as he addressed the 'End of Times' emergency. He called on all God's children to pray for victory of truth and righteousness over fear, hate, and Muslim extremism.

"Since 9/11 Islamic terrorists have carried out more than 30,954 deadly terror attacks, including 214 attacks with 1,552 homicides just during the month of May around the world. We should call this out for what it is. It is most certainly a war of religion. Extremism is a religion that calls for the extermination of 'infidels' outside their faith, specifically Jews and Christians. It's a religion that calls on its soldiers to shout 'Allahu Akbar' ('Allah is supreme' in Arabic) as they behead, rape, and murder in the name of radical Islam.

"This worldwide radicalization is only increasing with the advent of the internet and social media."

Reverend Graham closed. "I'm urging all within the sound of my voice, to do as Jesus did and forgive. To pray that God would give our president, our Congress, and our Senate wisdom, and the courage to do what is right for our nation, and not what's politically correct. My prayer has been for the United States and the United Kingdom to wake up before it is too late. That day has now come. God help us."

The stadium crowd joined him in a swelling crescendo, arms waiving, shouting out the gospel from the stadium to the streets, to the television audience, to the world. Franklin Graham, in most likely his greatest moment, bowed his head, reciting Isaiah 40:31.

But those who hope in the Lord will renew their strength.
They will soar on the wings of eagles.
They will run and not grow weary,
They will walk and not be faint.

The Secretary of Defense, watching Reverend Graham's broadcast on a side screen, turned to his boss, "Mr. President, the shit is about to hit the fan, Sir."

TOUCHDOWN, YELLOWSTONE GEOLOGY COMPLEX.

AC huddled with Dan, "Have the medics get everyone into Christie's lab. They can tend to them there. How's that shoulder holding up?"

"I'll live."

"Good, we have work to do."

Toad echoed, "Now we're talking. Let's kick some ass. Let's stop this thing. What's the plan?"

"Toad, do you remember that sonar guy in the submarine who could cancel out the sonar probes of the battle ships hunting us?"

"Sure do. We slipped right under their noses, slick as snot on a doorknob."

"Toad, you're foul." Christie volunteered.

191

He rolled his eyes at Christie with his best Arkansas possum eating grin as she continued to tend to Dan Shield's shoulder wound.

AC turned to Christie. "Ignore him. I have an idea."

"Christie, can you get on your computer and simulate two opposing waves meeting each other at the same speed and frequency?"

"I suppose so, but you need to give me more to work with here."

"If I remember my advanced math class in sonar school, two opposing impulse waves of equal strength cancel each other out. I'm talking about a way to neutralize Kamal's bomb blast and stop the eruption. We detonate a simultaneous directional explosion at the opposite side of the volcano. The super dense basalt bedrock of the earth's crust will direct both blasts toward the liquid center of the chamber. If we get this right, the shock waves should theoretically neutralize each other, right?"

Ten minutes later Christie had her program up and running, and it worked, in theory.

Dan spoke with the spark of an idea crystalizing in his mind. Christie, "Can you pull up an overlay of those bore holes and motion monitors you and Dr. Ainslee told me the about the last time I was here?"

AC took it all in, realizing his idea just might be possible. "Yeah, baby!"

"Dan, call Washington. Tell them we have a plan to stop this thing but we're going to need top security clearance to do the job."

Dan made the call, handing the phone to AC.

"Major Collins, this is the President in the situation room. We put you on speaker, so everyone is in the loop. What do you need?"

"Sir, I need a small nuclear bomb."

"What did you say?" The sound of quiet laughter could be heard in the background.

"A nuclear bomb, Sir. If we can insert a large enough charge of our own to detonate from the opposite end of the lava chamber, we may be able to neutralize Kamal's blast."

"Mr. President, I need to know if it's true that we have tactical nuclear weapons hidden in our ICBM sites, those tactical nuclear weapons we were going to use against Russian assault troops in the case of an invasion."

"Let me put one of the Joint Chiefs on the line."

No one was laughing now.

"Yes Major, but nobody was supposed to know about that. The MK-54 SADM (Special Atomic Demolition Munition) is a one-hundred-twenty-five-millimeter tactical field artillery device with an explosive nuclear yield of two kilotons."

Holding his hand over the phone, AC asked Christie, "How big are those monitoring bore holes of yours?"

"One hundred forty-millimeters."

AC jumped up from his chair, pumping his fist in the air, "Now we're cookin'."

"Sir, where is the nearest ICBM storage silo to Yellowstone?"

"About thirty air minutes away."

"Can we send our helo to get one of those MK 54's, and a nuclear engineer?"

"I'll do you one better, Major. We have assets on that site. Our bird will cut your operational down time in half, time you don't have to waste."

"Thank you, Mr. President, General. We'll be back to you within the hour with a game plan."

It was an exceptionally long half hour before the helo arrived with the MK-54. The medics used the time to attend to everyone's wounds. Coffee and sodas were passed around. It was a solemn group waiting to see if fate would give them the time they needed to execute the new plan. At any moment, the super-heated titanium shield on The Sword of Allah could fail and all would be lost in an instant.

Dan Shields sat beside AC and quietly, awkwardly, asked him, "How well do you boys know Christie?" Hoping inwardly, he hadn't asked a question he didn't want an uncomfortable answer to.

AC shot him THE LOOK, and in a loud voice replied, "What kind of question is that Shields? We're all likely to get blasted back to the Stone Age and you want to know if you have competition?"

Dan immediately regretted his question. Jealousy did not fit him well.

"Hey, Toad. Agent Shields here is asking about Christie's love life. Shit, Shields. Toad and I have loved her for years. She sets the bar pretty high, 'cuz neither of us measured up."

Patting his shirt pocket where he kept their photo safe, he continued. "She's been with us in some of the most exotic places this world has to offer, but she'd rather live in the mountains eatin' granola bars and drillin' holes in volcanoes. She ain't happy, we ain't happy, am I right Toad?"

Toad gave Shields his best junkyard dog scowl.

Christie blushed, slightly amused with a knowing smile. "Thanks a lot, AC. And I got your back, too!"

The mood changed back to serious business when they heard the whirl of helicopter blades approaching.

With no time for formalities, AC and Dan Shields up-linked communications and the Yellowstone lab computers to the Situation Room in the White House. All eyes and ears were riveted on the big screen.

Christie explained the plan to stop Kamal's eruption of Yellowstone to the nuclear engineer and to Washington simultaneously.

"We use seismic tomography to study the volcano, sending small dynamite blasts into the ground and reading their seismic signatures. These small shock waves travel at different speeds through different materials, faster through hard rock, slower through the liquid magma. Each monitor in the park has its own recording frequency."

"OK, I got that, but—" The engineer looked puzzled.

"I'm getting there, just follow me here. Every sonar man and commander in the submarine service knows there is a spot where two sonar signals meet and neutralize each other. It's called the null and it's a perfect place to hide from others. The detonation and resulting shock wave of Kamal's bomb will be traveling a thousand miles an hour through the molten lava, so a second charge needs to detonate almost simultaneously with Kamal's bomb if there is to be any chance of canceling the shock wave."

The President interrupted. "How do we know our bomb won't set off the eruption? What if Kamal's bomb fails and ours sets off the damn thing?"

"Kamal's bomb won't fail, Sir." The nuclear engineer explained. "Titanium melts at three thousand twenty degrees Fahrenheit. Dr. Albright tells me Yellowstone's magma averages around twenty-four-hundred degrees. Heat sink will gradually degrade the internal trigger mechanism on Kamal's RA-115. It will vaporize the surrounding material with sufficient corrosive force to the same effect as activating the original triggering device.

"Supposing you're right, how do you time that thing?"

"I'll rig the Mk-54 with a frequency trigger to detonate when the sensor, midway across the park's diameter, detects the approaching shock wave from Kamal's bomb. I'll lower it on the electric winch Dr. Albright used to lower temperature gauges and the chemical analysis 'smell testers' that record the chemical composition of the volcano's magma. We should be operational in another thirty minutes, Sir."

The President looked around the Situation Room and asked, "Well, why can't that thirty-six thousand atmosphere pressure Dr. Brian Hodges warned us about, spout out of that bore hole? Why don't Dr. Albright's test bores cause an eruption?"

"Sir, the bore holes are an insignificant pin prick to a volcano of this magnitude. Getting lava to the surface though a bore hole would be like pushing asphalt through a soda straw."

The Situation Room back in Washington remained tense, waiting for word of a successful placement of the counter device. Behind them loomed a large map showing in multi-colored shades the volcanic plume of destruction anticipated from a Yellowstone eruption; two thirds of America would be buried under a smothering blanket of ash and death.

"Mr. President, the second charge is positioned. All we can do now is wait."

"How long? When will we know?"

"Mr. President, if Dr. Albright's numbers are correct, and I believe they are, I would project heat sink will have breached the bomb's titanium shell twenty-four hours from the time Kamal threw himself and the bomb into Yellowstone's caldera. Given the time it took for our people to get back to the surface and back to this lab—"

"The time man, how much time!"

"Sir, within the next hour the world will know if there is going to be any North American tomorrow."

Everyone in the Situation Room shared the same thought; Redemption or Armageddon, which would it be?

A silent, ghostly pal fell over those assembled to watch the turn of fate's final card. Shaken hands, unable to get a phone call through the pandemonium, wrote hasted notes to loved ones. Some in the secretarial pool sat at their desks silently weeping, unable to call out, hug their families, or say their goodbyes. Those with influence ran a shuttle of helicopters to nowhere.

The Yellowstone lab triage medics tended to wounds suffered in the inner earth battle with Kamal and his martyr squad.

Hardened SEALS cleaned and rechecked their weapons. Dan Shields brushed off a medic. "If an hour is all we got, what difference will it make?"

Out of hearing of his comrades, Toad Rawlings made a call to his estranged father.

"Whatcha doing there, Toad?" AC asked.

"Just tying up loose ends, brother. Hell, I can't get through. And even if I could, he's probably too drunk to answer the phone. I can't leave the party without saying goodbye."

AC gave his buddy a passing nod and a pat on the shoulder.

Christie wandered over to sit closely beside Dan and wrapped her hands in his.

"That was sweet; what you said back there."

"Christie, you never know what you've missed until it's too late. A job's a job, but it's not all there is to this life. We seem to have found something neither of us expected. If we make it out of this mess—"

Christie interrupted, "I know." Her eyes said what words could not.

She continued. "I keep thinking about Dr. Ainslee and all he survived in the war, only to be killed in so horrible a fashion."

"Hell, he was killed forty-five years ago and just didn't know it. Damn fine man!"

Toad hollered over the din, "Hey AC, think we'll ever get a chance at some of that trout fishing you promised me?"

"Don't know, Ronnie. My guts in knots. I'll be happy to see the next ten minutes on this side of eternity."

Yellowstone Park was eerily quiet. The always constant breeze dropped to a stand-still. Birds fell silent. The entire world stood still as everything alive awaited the next turn of history's page. Then, ever so slightly, Yellowstone Lake started to vibrate. Milling buffalo stampeded in aimless terror.

A muffled whumph from multiple detonations deep within the earth could be felt through the soles of the feet. Old Faithful shot steam a quarter mile high, while Yellowstone Lake heaved upward. The Yellowstone River began to flow backwards, and fish were jumping desperately onto dry land, flapping about to escape some distant instinctive memory. Any more stress and the ceiling of the magma chamber would collapse with apocalyptic effect. Hundreds of millions of gallons of river water falling into the magma chamber would boil instantly, unleashing the thirty-six-thousand-ton atmospheric pressure of the volcano like a giant pressure cooker bomb, the Boston bombing by a factor of billions.

In the Washington Situation Room, the big screen connected to Yellowstone's monitoring systems showed in 'real time' the nearly simultaneous detonations. Both nuclear blasts, seen on screen as orange fireballs, deflected from the harder basalt walls of the magma chamber, racing toward each other at supersonic speeds. Bar graphs measured the on-rush of Kamal's Armageddon in graphic spikes. The energy pulses of both explosions crashed into each other in overlapping rings of red and orange, and began to collapse, as wasted waves upon the beach. They then retreated like the last ripples of a cooling pot of boiling water on the stove.

The meaningless concept of time seemed to drag on forever. Whitened knuckles gripped chair arms and sweat beaded foreheads awaited a fate now beyond control; one minute, five, ten, then quiet. The deep rumbling faded away. Monitors went silent. Yellowstone Lake calmed to a mild shimmer; a shaggy buffalo pondered his own reflected image as the river returned to its course.

Untenable stress broke slowly into sighs of relief, then smiles, and finally high fives all around the White House Situation Room and the Yellowstone lab.

Armageddon would have to wait for another day.

The entire world exhaled a unanimous sigh of relief, with one exception. The cheering and demonstrations in the streets of Islamabad faltered and dispersed. Allah's new reign would not be forthcoming today. Abu Aziz slammed down the phone and cursed the Great Satan, swearing revenge.

Back in the lab, Christie gave both AC and Toad a lingering kiss, then turned to Dan Shields and took his hand. "So, what do FBI agents do for fun when they're not saving the world from apocalyptic terrorists?"

Smiling for the first time in weeks, Dan put an arm around Christie's shoulder as they turned toward the door.

AC and Toad both shook their heads,

"Yeah, yeah, same ole Christie."

Toad turned to AC. "I guess you didn't do so bad for a jarhead Marine. You can come on back to the SEALS if you ever want a real job."

"When squids fly! Hey Toad, you ever think about that ranch we were going to buy?"

"Yeah, day-dreaming about that place got me through some tough times. Two tours of this shit, you know."

"Me, too. I wonder what a ranch like that would cost?"

"Oh, about this much." Toad pulled a diamond the size of a lemon from his pocket.

"Sumbitch, I was thinking the same thing." AC pulled a similar hog-choker from his pocket, too.

"But mine's bigger!"

They grinned and shook hands.

"We'll name it The Brimstone Ranch."

"Roger that!"

"And, Toad, you still got no game with the ladies!"

CHAPTER 19: L' EGRESS

Fate, again, interceded to put the lives of Dan Shields, Christie Albright, AC, and Toad on different paths to recovery from the stress and injuries suffered in their inner earth battle to defeat Kamal Rashid's jihadist Armageddon.

Abu Aziz, too, had his own moment of reflection. Islamabad, Pakistan, at a morning meal of dates and cheese followed with strong Arab coffee, Aziz and his cadre of zealots met to plan Allah's revenge against the Great Satan for his heretical thwarting of world-wide jihad. Abu's phone, quietly, and unbeknownst to its owner, was streaming a GPS signal to a silent messenger. The return message ringing back to the phone screen read, "Return to sender." Jumping to his feet, Aziz peered out from under his canvassed retreat to meet the whistle of the incoming ordnance.

Dan Shields took a three-month leave of absence from the FBI to heal his shoulder wound and tend to Christie's rehabilitation. In his absence he was quietly vetted for the eventual position of Director of the FBI.

Christie soon resumed her research at Yellowstone, though the loss of her dear friend, George Ainslee, left a void in her life that stole the passion from her work. With Dan now back full time at the Boston Bureau, she and Dan struggled to keep their budding love alive from two thousand miles apart, taking brief trips away to reinforce their bond. Trips throughout the American South held a particular attraction to them because of the rich history and the subdued lifestyle Southerners were known for. Since Christie grew up near Columbia, South Carolina, Savannah, Georgia, and Charleston, South Carolina were frequent destinations.

AC and Toad found themselves mired in a three-month battle with the IRS over the diamonds they pocketed from the Dragon's Mouth. Assayed at over $3 million, the IRS argued they were property of the United States Treasury, and should be confiscated, or in the alternative, taxed at market value. Declining either option, AC and Toad managed to engage the IRS Dick in a conference call with the White House, whereupon Dick was promptly instructed to go find someone else to hassle. The Brimstone Ranch was good to go. Christie's boys, while still on leave, enjoyed several weeks of trout fishing and exploring their new hooch on the Snake River in Wyoming before being called back to active duty.

AC Collins was given his choice of any duty station he wanted. He chose the Marine Corps Air Station, Beaufort, South Carolina because it was a short hop to anywhere east of the Mississippi River. In his new role as a Flight Instructor, he began to develop battle tactics using Naval and Air Force assets, such as the new Strike fighter and the battle tested and proven A-10 Thunderbolts, affectionately known in the community as Warthogs, in configurations previously considered heretical in military hierarchy.

Master Chief Toad Rawlings chose to continue to do what he did best. He loved the clandestine lifestyle of secretly keeping the bad guys in check. No glory, no big paycheck, no personal relationships tying him down. Yet secrecy and plausible deniability came with a price. A mission enacted to sever ties between eastern terrorists and Central American socialists resulted in his entire team being betrayed, then decimated in the deep, vastness of the Amazon jungle. No headlines, no rescue, no recovery. Rawlings and his team were unofficially listed, off the books, as MIA. So deep undercover was the mission that not even SEAL protocol allowed a hunt for their lost teammates. Dan, Christie, and AC were devastated.

Nearly a year after the destruction of The Sword of Allah a Presidential ceremony took place at the White House to honor those who gave so much of themselves to save America's future from the rule of tyranny. The President spoke of the uncommon bravery of common citizens to meet threats and challenges which appear impossible to accept.

"Since we were all in this together, and all worked as a team to neutralize the greatest threat to our national survival, I think it is appropriate to celebrate this occasion together."

Major Allen Carter, AC Collins, and Master Chief Ronnie Theodocius Toad Rawlings were awarded Medals of Honor, along with the rest of the SEAL Team. Family members of those lost in the effort accepted posthumous awards, while Master Chief Rawlings' award would be held until his MIA status was resolved, unofficially, of course.

Doctor George Ainslee was posthumously awarded the Presidential Medal of Freedom for his heroism under the harshest of conditions. The award was presented in a small glass-fronted box, painted black.

With the stipulation that his service would only be in effect for the remainder of the Presidential term, FBI agent Dan Shields was sworn in as the new Director of the FBI. His new bride, Dr. Christie Albright, held the Bible on which he swore his oath.

To put an exclamation, point on the enormity of the day, a formation of Marine Corps fighters from MCAS Beaufort, joined by a lone A-10 Warthog from Tucson, Arizona, roared overhead to a chorus of 'God Bless America' played by the US Navy band.

After the ceremony, the President pulled Dan Shields aside.

"Dan, you and I could use a couple of special operators, off the books, if you know what I mean. This international terrorism problem isn't going away anytime soon. I have a shit-pot full of trouble spots to deal with. I need results without too much scrutiny. I want you to think about a small team who can get results without splitting hairs on political correctness."

"Sir, I believe I may have an idea. I know what buttons to push."

A couple of days went by while Dan formulated a proposal for the President. Calling Major Collins to his new office, he didn't give him time to take off his cover.

"C'mon, AC. We have a meeting at the White House in thirty minutes. And just so you know, we never left this building." True to his word, there was no one to greet them

GIBBES McDOWELL

at the White House, nor was there any log entry of their presence. A junior staffer wordlessly escorted them to a small comfortable working office next to the Oval Office. The lights were off, except for one forlorn desk lamp.

As they entered, the President greeted them both with an extended hand, the other holding a small snifter of brandy. "It's good to see you again, gentlemen." He motioned for them to take seats in front of a paper-strewn desk.

"Major, I'll get right to the point. You're aware of the multitude of problem people in the world who feel strongly that they should be allowed to conduct their dirty business without scrutiny or accountability. Conventional diplomacy and limited military actions don't get the job done or are too costly in innocent lives lost and the negative kind of PR I really don't need. I've asked Director Shields to recommend a small team of patriots under your command who can act in situations that get real, actual results.

The President handed AC an open file folder labeled TOP SECRET and paused to sip his brandy.

AC read the bullet points, then placed the file on the edge of the desk. "Mr. President, Director Shields, what you're proposing is either treasonous folly or profound leadership."

AC paused for almost a minute while the President studied his nearly empty snifter and waited for AC to think it through.

"Mr. President, I accept your proposal, but only on the condition that I alone can select my team. I'm sure there are exceptional people who will jump at the chance to serve their country. But, Sir, there is no hope of making it work without Master Chief Rawlings as my wingman. Redneck

205

sum bitch went and got himself MIA for some raggedy-assed drug deal gone sour."

Then, in the silence of the room came a voice from a chair in the shadows behind them…

"Don't be so sure about that, jarhead…"

DRAGON'S MOUTH

CREDITS

Colonel George B. Utter (US Army Ranger)
Lt. Justin Besinger (US NAVY SEAL)
CWO4 Charles L. Jones (US Marine Corps)
Colonel Ross Roberts, (US Marine Corps, Retired)

DRAGON'S MOUTH

ABOUT THE AUTHOR

Since "Driftwood Unmasked" debuted in October 2018, Gibbes married his best friend, Fleetwood, to whom "Dragon's Mouth" is dedicated. His success with his first novel brought a loyal fan base who encouraged Gibbes to write more novels. A consummate storyteller, Gibbes created "Dragons Mouth", then went to work on two follow-on novels. The first of these, "The Eocene Event", will follow "Dragon's" beloved cast of characters on their next great adventure.

COMING NEXT FROM GIBBES MCDOWELL:

"THE EOCENE EVENT"

Hidden in plain sight for eons lays a terrifying secret desperately sought by rogue pharmaceutical and hostile government agents pursuing biological weapons. With its origin unknown to modern science, and genetically resistant to all attempts to contain it, the freed ancient killer begins a relentless march seaward toward a biological cataclysm. Patriots, driven by truth and unselfish honor, have 72 hours to prevent the next Eocene Event…